ELLA

and

The Tree of Mira

By Raffaella Corcione Sandoval

and Theodore J. Nottingham

Translated by Theodore J. Nottingham

Printed in the United States

To my Eternal Love Joshua

To my Master Sri Sathya Sai Baba

To my grandmothers Raffaela and Juanita: the past

To my daughters Cristina and Alessia: the present

To my grandchildren Aurora and Francescarama: the future

To my faithful Apollo and Zeus

To Ted: "toujours ensemble"

ELLA and The Tree of Mira

PREFACE

By Gianni Piettella

When asked if I wanted to write a preface to the novel by Raffaella Corcione Sandoval, I confess to having fallen from the clouds and to have been surrounded by doubt.

I know and appreciate the Italian-Venezuelan artist and her metaphysical pictorial and sculptural works and I was aware of her spiritual depth and her general knowledge of deep languages and mystical religions but I did not know of her writing skills and above all of her articulate understanding of esoteric doctrines.

'Ella', in fact, is not a simple novel but a powerful fresco that weaves together the author's biography and the 'magical' encounter with the American scholar Nottingham, co-author of the literary work, with the re-reading of sacred texts, from the New Testament to the so-called apocryphal Gospels, the scrolls of Qumran, the essays of Baigent, Lincoln and Leigh, the teachings of Sai Baba, and even the doctrine hidden in the folds of the religion of the Pharaohs.

A combination that, far from being a potpourri, is consistent in philosophical and spiritual investigation as it successfully attempts to restore unity to multiplicity, to govern syncretism by bringing chaos back to cosmos, through a red thread of esoteric wisdom.

Esotericism and love as a code are the two main features of Ella's story.

How much confusion occurs around esotericism, misinterpreting it with occultism. While the latter claims through magical arts to modify nature and the laws of physics that govern it, esotericism points to an 'inner', secret doctrine, the prerogative of initiates, based on symbolic knowledge that refers to the unity of the earliest archetypes.

Corcione Sandoval has knowledge of profound, symbolic and mystical languages and has skillfully seasoned the novel, telling a story which, from the power of an Egyptian amulet, leads through Miriam of Magdala to the Moma of New York, along a tale of sacred and profane love between the Elect and the Divine, between the Yin and Yang, between the death and resurrection of the Rabbi Yeshua.

Love is the keystone. It is between Miriam and Yeshua, it is between Ella and Nottinghill, it is between Ella and her daughters and between Ella and her friend Angelica.

They are partly different loves, on different levels of existence, but all united by an idea of time and space that transcends the consumerism of today which burns every relationship in the bonfire of narcissistic vanity.

Love becomes the code by which Yeshua communicates with the world, and his world is Miriam. She is destined through love to profound teaching, to the pedagogy of the doctrine of the man who makes himself King, of the Vitruvian man, measure of all things, not as a ruler of the world, but as one with the world, part of an integral pantheism.

It is love that makes the Miriam of the novel the guide of the apostles and of the disciples of Christ the Essene, it is love that Ella finds in the lotus flower which seals the book of wisdom, it is love that makes the Ella's daughters understand the originality of the mother, her eccentricity with respect to superficial normality.

Ella is truly a beautiful book that can be read in one go but that requires many readings to grasp the multiplicity of meanings and symbolic textual planes.

It is a neatly woven story, an artist ready for the inauguration of her work at the Moma in New York who, in her dressing room, receives a book as a gift, apparently from an unknown admirer.

In fact, the book is a story of initiation, of a transmission of ancient knowledge, of a mystical knowledge, through love, sacrifice, regeneration, pain, resurrection.

And the love in real life between Corcione and Nottingham, so delicate and profound, is not only a background but is the true protagonist who in backlight becomes heir to the mystical union of the Magdalene.

This is a book that could be the screenplay of a film, except that the greatness of its dialogues would risk simplification as a blockbuster, capable of making people reflect, unleash questions, undermine certainties, sow doubts, feed curious and ready minds.

Exactly what a good book must do.

INTRODUCTION

By Theodore J. Nottingham

This book is a synthesis of multiple styles integrated in a completely original way. It is biography, intuition, wisdom, revelation, narration generated through the creativity of the artist Raffaella Corcione Sandoval with my literary contribution.

Combining current and past life experiences with timeless insights, worthy of the great masters of spirituality, the reader is taken on a journey that will surely surprise and be cause for reflection. The work is articulated on several levels where sacred writings meet narratives with new perspectives. But the greatest surprise of all lies at the heart of the book.

It won't take long for all the elements to refer to the life of the central character.

Raffaella Corcione Sandoval is known for her multifaceted contemporary art in which she makes use of the semiotics of art. In this book, she reveals that her talent knows no limits and brings that creativity and originality into the literary form.

This book is a veiled biographical work, and offers the reader an unprecedented look through an intuitive and mystical portrait that will not be forgotten.

ELLA

by Raffaella Corcione Sandoval

and Theodore J. Nottingham

He slowly slid his fingers through his beard, an old habit when he wanted to reflect deeply. He couldn't be late. He had worked so hard over the last two years to be on time for this event. Surely the lack of punctuality in landing would not hinder the meeting with the one who had made his heart beat again, bringing him back to life. By nature, he was a man who did not show his emotions when excitement took over. But this moment in his life was completely unexpected and went beyond his control.

He picked up a small package that he had placed on the seat next to him, as it was fortunately empty. The package was simple, containing a book he had worked on in an atmosphere of magical passion as never before despite the many books he had published. A thin red cord was tied around the package, fixed by a seal in red wax with the engraving of a "fleur de lis". The result was elegant and symbolic against the light

11

brown background of the wrapping paper, a very essential and contemporary packaging, perfect for what it contained. He held the package against his chest as he looked out the window of the plane. He felt as if he had flown his whole life through such a vastness of turbulence before reaching this moment. Nothing could stop him now, not even the thunder in the sky.

At that moment, the grey clouds opened and beneath him was a light blue space. He couldn't help but smile. Before these last two years there had been darkness, uncertainty and despair, leading to resignation. Then, one day, a message suddenly changed the scenario around him and wonderful new possibilities appeared.

The plane shook as it passed through the turbulence, but the man was completely unaware of what was happening around him. Finally, he heard the airplane's wheels come down and, a few moments later, the loud breaking.

Being on time had always been important to him, almost in an exaggerated way. Even for the simple circumstances of life, he always made sure that his timing was right. Being ahead of schedule assured him of punctuality. But tonight in New York he had an appointment with destiny that was too important. It had all started out in a most unusual way and he never imagined that it would lead him to what was happening here and now.

Far from his isolated house, he had arrived in one of the largest cities in the world for the most important event of his life: looking into her eyes.

People slowly came out of the plane, exhausted and relieved by the fact that the long flight was finally over, but he passed in front of all of them, moving quickly. He was soberly dressed in a dark brown suit, the color of the Franciscan tunics, and this made him feel at ease.

The airport is one of the most exciting and chaotic places in the world, filled with thousands of unknown people of all races who meet only to never see each other again.

Dozens of shops line the vast corridors, each with its own marketing image in continuous and unstoppable competition.

An infinite variety of lights, decorations and writings sought to attract passers-by with all the most advanced techniques of digitalized psychological speculation.

The noise of the crowd is like the deafening buzz of a beehive that gradually becomes an echo, leaving one's thoughts to emerge undisturbed. Arabic music and a few meters ahead of the last success of Alvaro Soler. The scent of the new chick burger... and at the end of the moving walkway, the smell of the curry of an Indian restaurant... But he walked straight ahead, passing unnoticed.

All around him was a whirlwind of people calling friends or family, with smartphones of all brands and sizes, even children possessed them and played video games, some laughing, others arguing. He moved through the chaos with a stable presence like a column of silence and determination. In his hand, he carried the small package close to him.

Coming out of the airport, he immediately raised his hand to stop a taxi, and a yellow car pulled over. He entered quickly, said just a word to the driver, eager to collect his thoughts before reaching his destination. He looked at the package in his hand as if it were a Qumran manuscript, then he looked at the crowd on the sidewalks along the way. He thought about what their reaction would be if they knew what he had discovered. He knew that his research had led him to a revelation that would upset many of the earth's powerful with their rigid beliefs rooted in a past that had lost value along the way. Others would rejoice at the new revelations that would finally shed light on all that they had imposed on the masses of believers. Still others would immediately try to make it a new cult or worse. He didn't want to think about what could happen to her if his discovery were made public, but he knew what it meant for him and his life. There was no turning back. Everything would be different from now on.

***

A woman sat in a dressing room, all alone. The lights were low, generated by small lightbulbs around the mirror in which she was staring at herself, a ritual important to her because it was the most tangible way to find herself in moments like this with her beloved Joshua. Soon it would be time to go downstairs for the biggest event of her career as an artist. Her works were to be presented in a great exhibition so anticipated by the media and journalists who were waiting with great excitement to meet one of the most intriguing contemporary talents in the art world. She had struggled for a long time for this moment. It was her artistic dream, to affirm her professionalism, to be at the Moma in New York City.

Her beautiful features were slightly touched by the passing of the years and the painful vicissitudes of her personal life, but still full of charm and mystery. This evening, the euphoria that she should have experienced had left ample room for a veiled sadness. In another part of the building could be heard the noises of workmen preparing for the vernissage. She wore a special style, designed by herself since her passion for fashion had confirmed her as a designer since her youth. It was an amaranth-colored suit, a color she loved very much, formed by cigarette pants in pure Indian silk and a long jacket equal in fabric and color, completely closed to the waist by a row of small buttons and open in four panels. She liked to walk in trousers that highlighted her slender legs. She wore a long, thin red silk rope around her neck from which hung an imposing, authentic amulet, a turquoise and enamel scarab from the Ptolemaic period which she had owned for many years because it was the last gift of her paternal grandfather, a jewelry dealer, before he died. She really wanted to wear it because she perceived that all the positive energies were attracted by it, creating an electromagnetic field around her, as she inevitably drew the gaze of anyone who would be in front of her. She was undecided whether to wear a pair of beautiful high-heeled sandals that would make her look slimmer or very low-colored flats that made her feel barefoot as when she walked around the house at ease.

She hadn't done her makeup yet as she could do it professionally in a short time because she had always done it herself. As a teenager she had a sense of having a proportionate and pleasant face but she had never liked her face naked. And her hair? What a disaster her hair was, always worn long and a bit wild.

This was the Vernissage of the Year, but as usual, she did not want to go down those stairs. She had worked so hard on her artistic goals all her life, sometimes feeling like Don Quixote, always alone. Her sense of honesty and purity had prevented her from making compromises with the art system, because her work was mystical and non-speculative. Alone with her determination, her broad vision and her faith, she had climbed the steep mountain that had brought her to this moment of success for a very precise mission: Bringing the Gospel of Truth through the symbolism of Art in every corner of the world; and to motivate herself to reach a wide popularity in which she ironically defined herself as: Lady Picasso.

Her works had always been ahead of their time, new and original. She worked with the same clarity of purpose with which she lived her life. She was her Art.

So why did she want to run away? She wanted to go far from the crowds of people who showed off their culture in order to feel fulfilled among fellow artists, admirers and critics, who were often the same people.

Her natural shyness was a valid and little-known reason, given her friendly, cheerful nature. With every year that passed, she preferred more and more the tranquility of contemplation to the social scene, along with significant encounters with interesting people. Any artificial thing was for her anathema and made her absolutely allergic to fiction and false emotions.

She preferred the company of children and animals to the sumptuous reign of celebrities and the self-absorption of the media. Her paintings were imbued with this energy, this higher vibration in which she lived. Now she just wanted to be at home with her feet up and her beloved dogs lying next to her.

A knocking at her door took her away from her memories.

"Who is it?" she asked, forced to answer, wanting to be somewhere else.

Two smiling faces appeared as the door opened. They were her beloved daughters, here to rejoice with her at this important milestone and to support her psychologically. She was always happy when she could spend time with them under any circumstances.

Their first question was now part of a ritual: "Are you ready to show yourself?" but they immediately saw the state of bewilderment their mother was in. Like her, they had a strong natural sensitivity for perceiving the energies of those who came into contact with them.

This was a gift inherited and handed down from generation to generation through the women of the family in a royal bloodline. She had cultivated this gift in her daughters from a very young age and had never been able to hide anything of her life from them, not even her sentimental life. Cristiana and Benedetta had always been very close to their mother, accepting her original and adorable personality, which was sometimes difficult for them because it was seemingly childlike. Despite her total dedication to Art, she was first and foremost a mother and would sacrifice herself unreservedly for her children.

The daughters knew her artistic and spiritual soul well and often teased her with elegant irony that she seemed to live in another dimension, far from the practical things of life. At the same time, since her divorce, she had built her existence on her own and in her own way. Her daughters admired her very much for her inner strength and had drawn inspiration from it by shaping their approach to life with a positive attitude.

She had intentionally passed on to her daughters her interest in spiritual matters, knowing that the greatest legacy she could leave them would be "Faith."

Both had pursued this goal and it had taken them further than she could have hoped. Now Cristiana and Benedetta were facing her at the highest point of her career.

Seeing the joy in their eyes, she remembered a specific moment some twenty years before. It had become one of the motivating causes for why she was here now. They had been invited by an old and dear friend of the family to his beautiful and ancient Villa on the sea, near their residence. All the guests at the sumptuous New Year's Eve party waited, elegantly dressed and excited, to drink a toast to the arrival of the long-awaited year 2000. But unlike all the others, Ella was filled with a veiled melancholy. Her inner feelings contrasted sharply with the colors and festivities that surrounded her, highlighting her fragility.

She headed for a large window with a breathtaking view. The view looked out on the famous and beautiful gulf of her city, more illuminated than usual. The lights of the hill of Posillipo were all reflected on the sea below which, combined with the blue of the clear sky full of stars, seemed to be a "tableau vivant" of Van Gogh. At that moment Ella was alone and did her best not to cry.

Her daughter Benedetta noticed her and came over to hug her. It was a moment of special love between them. Her little girl was becoming a beautiful young woman. But what she remembered about that evening was the solemn promise she made to her daughter at the stroke of midnight amidst tears and cheers of glasses filled with Don Perignon. Benedetta had asked her to swear that with her work she would become famous because her works deserved to be known throughout the world for the important message they contained. Ella made that promise with all her heart, as promises for her became law, but that night it was something more, it was a sacred act. She kept this in mind for the rest of her life, on every occasion that she was applauded and recognized. At each vernissage, when her daughter arrived, she always said to her: "I did it for you...".

She was happy to show her that she had kept her promise in mind. Yet, her successes did not fully satisfy her despite the great completeness achieved through spiritual research and her natural mystical character. It would have been nice to be able to share her life with a special companion, an ideal man she had always hoped to meet, a man able to give her what it was so natural for her to give in Love: All or nothing.

"What's wrong, Mom?" Cristiana asked, always the first to speak between the two of them.

Ella would have liked to say "Nothing", but she had never been able to lie and so she simply looked at them. As sweet as ever, they ran to embrace her because the most important thing was enclosed in the embrace of the three of them together!

"I want to go home...".

"Mom! How can you say that? Being here is what you've always dreamed of!" Cristiana said with emphasis.

Benedetta, the most introverted of the two, turned to her sister and said calmly:

"You know she doesn't like being in the crowd."

"But the crowd is here to admire your work! They love you!"

Benedetta took her hand. A tear shone in Ella's eye.

"That's the reason, isn't it?" Benedetta asked thoughtfully.

Ella shook her head without saying a word. At this moment, she seemed to be the daughter rather than the mother.

"What then?" Cristiana asked, wondering why her mother was not enjoying the special moment. It made no sense to her. She knew how hard she had worked to reach this evening.

"You owe it to yourself, Mom," continued Cristiana. "You deserve it."

"Don't put pressure on her, Cristiana," said Benedetta, who was always the most understanding and tolerant of the two towards their mother. "Give her time!"

"There is no more time! People are coming in right now."

At that moment, a gentle knock at the door caused her to turn around, thinking that someone would open it. Cristiana and Benedetta exclaimed in chorus "Asia!!!!" believing that their friend and sister Asia, an art historian and now a famous Ella loved as a daughter, had come from France.

They had shared with Asia important moments and stages of daily life and of the initiatory journey of which Ella felt she had been their first teacher. Only a few years before did Asia fulfill the dream of becoming a mother, without fear or prejudice. She brought into the world two wonderful twins, special beings that would help her to remain an eternal girl. Asia and her magical family could not miss this evening in New York because this artistic project, conceived by Ella after the tragic event of the Twin Towers, entitled DiaLogos, made up of eleven travelling exhibitions in search of harmony between opposites, they had begun together twenty years earlier.

Hearing no response, Cristiana got up quickly and walked towards the door, and like a bodyguard opened it only a few inches, wanting to protect her mother's privacy.

"What is it?" he asked.

A young man stood before her, impeccable in his role.

"I have...a package for the artist."

"I'll take it, thank you," said Cristiana, "I'm her daughter." She closed the door, and looking carefully at the package, she noticed the red thread fixed by the imprint of a seal in wax with a fleur de lis.

"What could it be?" she asked herself, recalling the importance that this ancient symbol had for her mother throughout her life.

"Maybe we should keep it for later," Benedetta suggested, looking at the time on her mobile phone.

Ella raised her eyes and immediately saw the red cord that surrounded the small packet.

"Let me see it," she exclaimed.

"You need to go down right away," said Cristiana, once again trying to convince her.

Ella's sweet eyes took on a more determined expression.

Cristiana knew that there was no arguing with her mother when that look appeared.

She gave it to her without discussion.

Ella took it in her hands with curiosity, trying to evaluate its energy, and something in her sensed that it was a very special gift. Her right hand instinctively went to the red thread around her neck and, sliding down, tightened around the cameo that was suspended there. It was an ancient and authentic scarab made of turquoise paste that entered exactly into her tightened hand.

Turning the package, she saw the seal with the symbol and an electric reaction went through her heart, like a flash, a glow that completely illuminated her. Her whole body responded to a mysterious call.

Raising her head, she looked at her daughters and smiled. Both realized that she needed to be alone for a moment and, without saying anything, they left the room, remaining outside the door.

Ella stared at the package for a moment before opening it. The lily always made her heart beat wherever she saw it reproduced. It had had a special meaning for her linked to unconditional love. She knew that it originated from the lotus flowers of ancient Egypt, which represented life and resurrection. The three stems curved to the left as if they had been brought to life by the breath of Hu, the Heavenly Sphinx, bearer of sacred knowledge. The hieroglyph that formed the original lily was a symbol of the Tree of Life.

She knew that this small package was somehow linked to that dream she had one night two years earlier.

She opened the package and found herself holding a book entitled "The Tree of Mira" written by a certain Jess Nottinghill!

"It's been two years..." she exclaimed out loud. On hearing her speak, her daughters entered the room again.

Cristiana bent down discreetly, enough to see the author's name.

"What does that mean, two years later?" Benedetta asked shyly.

"Two years...Since I sent the first letter...He has never replied in all this time...."

Cristiana put her arm around her shoulder.

"Forget it, Mom. This moment is the only one that counts now, you will read it when it's all over, or tomorrow calmly..."

"The dream..." said Ella.

"What dream?" Christian replied. "You've had so many...".

"So many special ones", Benedetta added. "We will make a book of them one day with all those you have transcribed."

"The dream..." Ella said again.

The sisters looked at each other. Then they both remembered at the same time which dream she was referring to. It was the last one in which the "voice" had spoken to her clearly and precisely about her future.

"Oh, that dream... that man," they said in unison.

"The indication of the voice was so clear..." whispered Ella.

"I know you never doubted your inner voice," said Cristiana with understanding.

"Never..." said Ella, excitedly.

"So, don't give up your intuition, just wait as long as you want, the people who visit the exhibition will wait for you!!! "said Benedetta with sweetness.

Cristiana and Benedetta left the room and descended the stairs leading to the main hall where the exhibition was held.

"Did you see the name of the author of that book?" Benedetta asked discreetly.

"I did."

"Of course you did," said Benedetta with a wink, knowing her sister well.

"Jess Nottinghill...Have you heard of him?" asked Cristiana.

"No."

"We need to find out who he is," said Cristiana insistently.

"Now?"

"Now!"

"But... the vernissage has begun," said Benedetta as she watched the growing crowd.

"Look on your iPhone," suggested Cristiana.

The sisters came down the stairs and headed for the guests who gathered around the paintings, eager for the event to begin. Among them, a young woman was looking for Cristiana and Benedetta. She turned and saw them, waved her hand in the air with enthusiasm.

"Look, it's Sofi!" Benedetta said with a big smile, greeting her.

Cristiana ran to meet her, happy to see their friend-sister and they hugged each other.

They had grown up together, knowing each other since childhood and they were happy that she had come from

Naples, Italy to honor their mother, her second mother, at this moment of her career.

"Where is she?" asked Sofí.

The sisters explained that she was still in her dressing room. They told her about a mysterious book that seemed so important to their mother. Sofí looked at them with an amused expression and said:

"We know what Ella is like!"

The three of them entered a corner of the room and Cristiana began to tell her what had happened.

Alone in the dressing room, Ella stared at the book she was holding in her hands, put on her glasses, opened it with trembling fingers and began to read.

The Tree of Mira

The Tree of Mira

Dedicated to Ella

The sun was high and blinding. Jerusalem, the Holy City, was full of life. The market was as crowded as every day and the sellers shouted their goods to passers-by. Large baskets carried on the heads of proud mothers were a reminder of the cradle in which Moses was found along the Nile. Visitors wandered into the crowd intoxicated by the scents of spices and flowers, wrapping themselves in the colorful silks suspended by merchants. But this day was a day that would never be forgotten, the day when history changed forever and, with it, the journey of the human soul.

A woman walked through the crowd, her gaze penetrated through everything going beyond it, barely noticing the world around her. She moved as in a dream, at a different rhythm from everyone she met. Her eyes seemed to be present, but in another dimension, and her features revealed a transcendent joy. More than joy, it was ecstatic awareness, because she still had her gaze fixed into the eyes of her holy man.

31

No one paid attention to her. The chores of daily life kept everyone buried in distraction and haste. In their unawareness, these people could not imagine that after the passage of this humble and radiant woman, embodying a greater reality, nothing would ever be the same again.

Her face still showed signs of the incredible grief that the days before had engraved in her soul. Within her there was a mysterious knowledge of what was to come. In the darkness before dawn on this day, she had received confirmation through the sound of her name.

"Miriam..."

She could still hear the sweet voice of her beloved resounding in her ears and spirit. It was with that one word that holiness would flood the world with its light. She walked quickly, returning to her friends after sharing what had happened with his mother who had not doubted her for a moment, and still feeling wrapped in her powerful embrace, she knew she would find them ready to listen.

She moved quickly in a labyrinth that she knew well, through narrow streets in the heart of the big city. The further she moved away from the market, the less shouting she could hear, letting emerge the women's songs in the ancient Aramaic language. Some buildings had high walls that shut out the sky, preventing the sun from illuminating the small houses she passed by.

This was a world in its own right, a city within a city. This was a place where her friends could not be identified by those who were looking for them. It was a community with its own rules, where people taught solidarity and brotherhood to their children, and everyone protected each other.

She walked through a code of silence set like a crown tiara, known only to the natives of the area worthy of wearing it from generation to generation.

She reached an external staircase, stopped for a moment to look around before climbing it all in one breath and without effort to find herself in front of a small wooden green door on the first floor, hidden from the road.

Before knocking, she closed her eyes for a moment and breathed deeply, placing here right hand on her belly. All her friends were there, those whom she really felt as such in her heart, for they had never dared to judge her because he always wanted her by his side. She knew she had no other such friends. Martha and Lazarus, even though blood related, did not always appreciate her behavior because they thought it was embarrassing.

Peter opened the door. They were all there, in the center of the room, some sitting on benches next to the table, others on stools, others on the floor. Their humble clothes had traces similar to graffiti, perfectly describing the night spent with him among the olive trees and the pain, the loss and the fear of the days of hiding. On their faces, the insomnia and the waiting had hollowed their eyes.

The murmur stopped instantly and everyone turned to her. They were happy to see her. This woman was the one who had brought them the most important news in history.

John said immediately:

"Miriam.... We prayed so much while we waited for your return."

She approached them and Andrew offered her his chair.

"What do we do now?" asked Peter.

She looked towards the small window to calculate the time from the position of the sun and the color of the sky, and answered.

"We wait...".

"What?" asked Matthew.

A barely perceptible redness warmed her cheeks but she added nothing else, because everyone knew the answer even though it was still incomprehensible to them.

"Can it really be like that?" Nathaniel thought in his heart.

John seemed to read his thoughts and turned to his brother, saying: "What did the Master tell us?"

"Three days..." whispered Andrew.

"But it was never clear what he told us," replied Philip with frustration. "How could we have imagined it?"

After a moment, Nathanael approached Miriam and asked her:

"Why did the Master choose you to witness his resurrection? And why did he choose you to receive the secret teachings?"

Miriam closed her eyes and let her thought arise from beyond her mind. Then, she responded slowly, letting every word incarnate from within her with spontaneous ease.

"When the One becomes the Two, the cosmic game of duality comes to life. When they meet, the two eternal, opposite, individual and evolved souls recognize each other because they have a common purpose.

The vibration of their cells becomes a magnet that inevitably attracts them to merge the two polarities and proceed in a new cycle of experiences to complete a mission established in the mists of time by the will and perfection of the One.

The level of communication of the two entities is mainly based on a vibrational Echo composed of a silence full of sounds, deafening for the many, which they acquire in their expansion and rearrange along their individual paths, creating compatible forms and colors, in the complex emotional universe from which the Word is born in its manifest word.

It was not only a transmission of secret oral teachings, but a sharing of confirmations, in which his foot entered perfectly into my imprint.

No one else could have approached his renewed appearance because he was totally intimate in his physical body, strengthened by the atomic radiance."

They let the words penetrate deeply into them. Everyone knew that they were coming from a very high place. After a moment, Peter asked:

"Why did the Master hide some of his Teachings?"

Miriam's gaze was directed toward the beam of light that entered through the window but seemed to look into a dimension invisible to others, and she said:

"His teachings were free and perfect, but not everyone who listened to him was at that moment."

Her word was a palpitating seed, scattered abundantly in arid fields ... and rain, which penetrated into the heart of each individual, broke through to make germinate the way, the truth and the new life on earth.

"Nothing happened secretly, everything took place in the sunlight, the sun that shines in every one of us and never sets."

"Why did he come?" asked Andrew.

"Creation is a manifestation that has exploded from what we know as the Supreme Good. It wanted to let itself go and overflow the banks of the Pythagorean Logic to affirm itself as the Power of Love, manifesting itself in Him, the Synthesis of Cosmic Radiation, as the highest example of divine and human incarnation."

The men listened to her breathlessly, immersing their hearts and minds in the meaning of her words.

"How did you perceive that this is what He is, that He is this Synthesis?" asked John.

"It is not a perception, it is a quiet consciousness that was born with me and is made concrete in Him."

Philip could not miss this rare opportunity to ask the question that burned within him since he first met the Master.

"Is he human or divine?"

"What is born of the flesh is flesh, what is born of the spirit is spirit, what is born of love is divine, He is the son of this triad and therefore of the Earth," she answered with profound knowledge.

Encouraged by Miriam's willingness to speak on these matters, Nathanael asked with emotion:

"Why do we exist?"

Miriam, looking with maternal love at all of them, answered:

"The Earth is a coveted and necessary star for the eternal intelligent spirit. Matter, in all its forms, contains within itself the interactive memory and allows the dualism of opposites to live fully, producing psychic and physical experiences necessary for the expansion of each individual consciousness in the conception of the One."

Matthew wanted to go further in this mystical revelation.

"Is the Creator Male or Female?"

She smiled: *"The quietness in which creation is immersed has been fertilized by an imperceptible breath of wind, giving life to the worlds: The Ma-trix."*

"Is he like us?" asked James, speaking for the first time without shyness. James had always been happy just to listen, but now he felt encouraged to receive answers from this woman who knew so much.

She said:

"He is like us in the body, like the father in the word, like the mother in essence."

John, leaning forward, almost on his knees, asked as if in prayer:

"Tell us what it means 'like the Father in the word'".

"He is like the father in the word because through his mind the Universal Logos makes itself accessible in concept, and translates itself into human communication."

"What is the Mother?" asked James, feeling in his question horizons of intuition that he would never have hoped to be able to approach again. It seemed to all of them that they were still before Him.

"The Mother is the supreme and expanding consciousness from which individual and universal identity blooms cyclically."

"What do you mean that in his essence he is like the Mother?" Matthew wondered, astonished at how such questions could be answered.

"He is like the Mother in essence because through her pattern she creates boundless new worlds in which Unconditional Love dwells, in its perfect psychic form, as a manifestation of that which grants everything and asks for nothing."

Once again, there was a pause as each man reflected on what he was hearing. But their zeal for knowledge and understanding made them unable to be silent.

"Why does wickedness exist?" Peter asked.

Miriam closed her eyes. The words she was about to speak came from deep knowledge.

"The experience of pain is the seal that certifies the origin of good. Without knowing the meaning of evil in all its forms, the Faith in which Good resides would not have developed."

"What is this seal?" he asked.

"The seal is the authentication of the aesthetics of pain. A special energy is produced by such an experience, which one must inevitably penetrate in order to access the truth!"

The disciples looked at each other, admiring what they heard.

"What does this experience want to accomplish in us?" John asked then, and his heart beat faster. His question was not simply intellectual speculation.

"He doesn't want anything," she said, *"he can't want anything, he just makes himself a mirror of our immensity and shows us the formula of love for opening the doors closed to the light, simply by an act of will."*

"What happens to us if we experience this light?" asked Philip, with eyes full of tears of joy in hearing these things.

"We become Kings," was Miriam's immediate response. These few simple words left them breathless.

After that response, the disciples remained silent for a long time. Those words had opened their hearts and minds to new realizations.

Then John spoke. "Miriam, you are in this light. Tell us which door did you enter?"

She turned to him and said calmly, from the depths of her being.

"From his eye, Royal Door of Eros."

"Tell us about this mystery," John asked quietly.

"God is love, joy, beauty, happiness, poetry. God is Eros, fullness, ecstasy, contentment, music, song, peace, harmony, faith... and much more. The Ego makes us believe that only through sacrifice, renunciation, mortification, guilt, anguish, melancholy do we atone for our sins and, unfortunately, even when we have overcome certain trials, we become dependent on pain.

It is only through the discipline of happiness that we obtain the connection with God".

John's eyes were full of wonder and hope, as if he had discovered beauty for the first time.

"Do you mean that we encounter God through joy?"

"God is absolute perfection, why would He make us suffer? We have not been able to understand how the divine laws work. God is Compassion and Forgiveness, not pain in the mind and mortification of the body. When that happens, God

is helping us to see that we are not on the right track with our thoughts."

The disciples looked at each other in silence, amazed at these words; they were at the dawn of a new understanding!

A sweet expression crossed Miriam's face, a manifestation of an inner light that was her very essence.

"We must truly believe that we are all One, we cannot distance ourselves from the path of growth of another soul, because we are part of its Karma, it is working to reach the heart of God with us. Each one of us is collaborating with this global growth and, when one of us understands this secret, it is our duty to be happy and we expand like an oil stain to point the way to a New Covenant of unity. To love ourselves is not enough, to love the other is not enough, to live in infinite joy is to love oneself and the other, this is the only antidote against the pain of humanity".

"Sister, tell us why our religious sages reject him."

"Because this power is priceless. No endless source of material wealth can take possession of it. They understood how penalizing the fear of the death of bodies is for man and they did not want the truth to be known to ordinary people

because in this way they would no longer have power as the only intermediaries between God and man."

"What is there beyond the bodies?"

"The All in nothingness".

A passing cloud darkened the room for a moment. Then the sun returned, sending a single ray of light through the window, illuminating a solitary chalice on the table, its shadow magnified and extended toward the ceiling, and everyone looked up. The door opened at the same time, and the disciples simultaneously looked in its direction. Miriam remained absorbed, in her guise of light, a new glow now emanated from her features: She knew it was him!

The disciples stood, amazed, as the Master entered. He raised his hand and in blessing them the room was filled with an otherworldly peace. His eyes turned to Miriam and he moved towards her as if she were the only one present. He stood in front of her and put his hands on her shoulders, staring deeply into her eyes.

"Miriam..." he said in a new voice.

She looked up and lost herself in him. Through his eyes she reached their alcove, and they burned with presence and intimacy.

They had always been ONE.

The disciples did not dare to speak as everything was impregnated with their electricity.

Their love was evident to all, an inexpressible love, beyond human understanding, but intensely embodied in their features, in their touch, in the subtle smiles that revealed the ecstasy of their encounters.

The silence was broken only by the common emotion. Some of them trembled at the sight of their beloved Master. Despite everything He had told them privately, they had never hoped to see him again, not even after Miriam had come to tell them what she had seen at the tomb that morning. They were astonished by his arrival. Not even the apparent normality allowed them to disguise this state of wonder, a leap from fear to joy without limits.

Andrew was the first to speak to break the spell. He wanted to do so like a child who, on the return of the Father, tells him everything that happened in his absence, without control.

"Miriam announced your promise to us and told us incredible things while we were waiting for you, Master."

The Master freed Miriam from his penetrating gaze and, as he always did, turned his loving eyes on them, looked at them one by one, and holding her hand, he smiled and nodded!

Philip came forward, trying to be closer to his Master.

"She told us about Creation..." he said excitedly.

John also came forward, so as not to lose sight of his eyes.

He went on to say, "Miriam says that creation is an explosive manifestation of what we know as the Supreme Good."

Peter continued:

"and...that in that explosion matter contains an interactive memory...".

The Master smiled and looked at Miriam. They exchanged a knowing gaze.

The disciples understood at that moment that there was so much more between the two of them unknown to them....

Matthew came forward.

"Tell us more, Master. Is matter eternal or will it be destroyed?"

The Savior said, "All nature, all formations, all creatures exist within one another, and they will be resolved again in their own roots. For the nature of matter is resolved in the roots of its very nature. Those who have ears to hear, let them hear".

Peter said to him, "Since you have explained everything to us, tell us also this: what is the sin of the world?"

The Savior said, "There is no sin, but you sin when you do things that are like the nature of adultery, which is called sin. That is why the Good has come among you, to the essence of all nature, to bring it back to its roots. "

Then he continued, "That is why you get sick and die, because you are deprived of the one who can heal you. Whoever has a mind to understand, let him understand. Matter has given birth to a passion that is unparalleled, that comes from something contrary to nature. Then a disturbance arises in his whole body. That is why I told you: be courageous, and if you're discouraged, be encouraged by the presence of the different forms of nature. He who has ears to listen to, listen to him."

When the Blessed One had said this, he greeted them and said, "Peace be upon you! Receive my peace in your hearts. Make sure that no one misleads you by saying, 'There he is, or "Here he is!' For the Son of Man is in every one of you! Follow his path! Whoever seeks him will find him. Go therefore from

47

here and proclaim the news of the Kingdom. See that you do not stipulate any rules beyond those which I have given you, and do not promulgate a code of laws as the legislator does, so that you will avoid being bound to them".

After saying these words, he left them.

They remained in silence, preoccupied and sorrowful. They wondered how they should go to the nations and proclaim the gospel and the news of the kingship of the Son of Man?

Someone with tears in their eyes whispered, "How can we go to the pagans and preach the gospel of the Kingdom of the Son of Man? If they have not spared him, how will they spare us?"

Then Miriam stood up, and said to her brothers: *"Do not cry and do not grieve, nor be irresolute, for His grace will be entirely with you and will protect you. For we praise his greatness, because he prepared us and made us His own."*

When Miriam said this, she calmed their hearts, and they began to discuss the words of the Savior.

Peter asked Miriam, "Sister, we know that the Savior loved you more than the rest of the women. Tell us the Savior's words that you remember and know."

Miriam answered, *"What is hidden from you, I will proclaim to you."*

"Why does the Master say that there is no sin in the world?" Peter asked, finding it difficult to hide his confusion.

Miriam replied: *"The Master says that there is no sin in the world because the world is our holographic creation. We are a projection of the Absolute Good and what we call sin is a condition of error in which the movements of our consciousness develop, influencing the psyche and finally the body, also causing physical pain. Everything is part of the path of the knowledge of Truth.*

Everything that makes us unhappy in any way and makes us suffer is a sign to indicate that we are not on the right path. All we have to do is analyze the cause and recognize the error. The error is given by the EGO, whether it comes from us or from the other, and because we are all ONE with him, as happened to him, it disguises itself and camouflages itself so as not to be recognized, even masking itself with our own features. My Beloved said quite simply: Do not do to the other what you do not want to be done to you; love your neighbor as yourself. Putting this simple rule into practice would make us all illuminated."

Nathanael asked, "How is it that the son of man is within us?"

"He is within us as each one of us is a child of the mother, He lives in us, breathes with us, dreams with us, suffers and

49

smiles through us, feeds on our love and we live through his love because everything is of the same substance as the father."

"Why then do we feel so separated if we are all of the same substance? Are we not individual creations, with our mind and our will making decisions for ourselves?" Philip wondered, confused in the face of these paradoxes.

Miriam answered:

"The big mistake is to suppose that we must lose our individuality to merge with the collective consciousness. But the reality is that in unity with the collective consciousness, we do not lose our individuality. Our enemy is the Ego, which claims its illusory identity in opposition to the unity of collective consciousness. When this happens, we feel alone. But the truth is that we are one with all that lives and does not live. We are not alone, we are one with everything. In that unity, we rediscover our individual Self within that collective consciousness. What we need to understand is that our individuality must not be confused with aloneness but must lead us to unity."

"So every soul is present to itself even in the beyond, isn't it? This means that we will not be alone even after our journey to heaven," said Peter with a voice betrayed by a slight tremble.

Miriam smiled and embraced their anxieties with her gaze, took a slow and deep breath and began to speak, looking intensely into their eyes:

"I saw the Lord in a vision and said to him: "Lord, I saw you today in a vision". He answered me and said to me, 'Blessed are those who have not wavered at my sight. For where the mind is awakened there is the treasure.'

And I asked him, "We know that you will let us rise to the kingdom of Light from where we came for the first time. And that is where we want to gather with you, so that we no longer feel orphaned in this world. But we don't know the way to go. Do not leave without revealing to us the invisible path that leads to the Father and that every soul must follow when leaving behind the mixture with matter on the day when the flesh loosens its grip.

He answered me: "Miriam, I will show you the way you must travel, so that on the day your brothers and sisters ask you for these things, you know what you and they need to know, so that we can be gathered together in the House of Light on high, from where all the first souls came.

First of all, know this: the way is simple, but it is not free. It winds through the seven celestial spheres, and each of them is jealously guarded by its guardian and toll collector, always

51

vigilant in receiving its due. But even though they are vigilant, it is possible to face them, provided that we know what words will allow you to overcome them.

"And he showed me in my vision the Redeemed Soul, the one who knows its origin and its destiny. That soul arose like a spark from a bonfire in the cold night. After she had detached herself from the limiting body of the flesh, she continued to rise until her soul reached the first of the Powers, whose name is Darkness, who spoke to her, "Do not proceed any further, transgressor! And the soul answered, "Why? What have I sinned against you? And the darkness answered, "In my kingdom without light, no one who lights the torch of knowledge is allowed to stay. Here we extinguish the sometimes painful light, so that all may return to the peaceful sleep of ignorance. And that soul answered, "No, darkness, those who sleep your sleep do so only because they ignore your cunning! But the Teacher has warned me of this! And so I escaped the Power of Darkness, rejoicing that I was free from another nature, that of worldly ignorance."

The disciples listened, absorbed by her words, amazed by the vision she shared with them.

"After a time that soul passed into the sphere of the Archons of Desire, which causes the natures to mingle and seeks to awaken in the fleeing soul the affection for those false delights that it has left on earth, so that it can return there. Desire itself was there, in an instant, talking to him and saying, "Who are you? And where do you come from?" And the soul said: "I am the seed of the living Father and I do not belong to this world. You will not prevent me, as I try, from returning to the place from which I came for the first time.

So he spoke to him. And Desire said to that soul: "I have never seen you come down, but now I see you coming up! What makes you lie? You are mine." The soul replied, "I have seen you, but you have not seen me, nor have you noticed me. You saw nothing but my robe, and you didn't recognize me." When she said these words, she left with great joy.

"Then she met the third Power, called Ignorance. She questioned the soul and said, "Where are you going? You are bound by evil. In fact, you are bound! Don't judge!" And the soul answered, "And who are you to judge me like that? I have not condemned you! Verily, I was chained to the flesh, and now I am free. I have not been recognized. But now I can recognize that the All is being deconstructed, both the earthly and the heavenly elements."

"When the soul had triumphed over the third power, it ascended and saw the fourth power, which assumed seven similarities. The first of the similarities is Darkness, the second Desire, the third Ignorance; the fourth is the Terror of Death; the fifth is the Kingdom of Flesh; the sixth is the illusion of the "Wisdom" of the flesh; the seventh is the wisdom of the angry person: the Pride of the Ego."

Miriam, who had closed her eyes when she spoke, opened them and looked at them, wrapped in a light that shone from her body.

"These are the Seven Powers that each of us must face. They question the soul: "Where do you come from, murderer? Where are you headed space traveler?" For its part, the soul replied, saying, "What kept me prisoner has been defeated, and what enveloped me has been disintegrated, and my desire has been fulfilled, and ignorance has expired. In the midst of the world I was freed from a world and, freed from a pattern of death, I received liberation from the celestial prototype, liberation from the chain of oblivion. From now on, I will win my way to that rest where no one talks about time, season, age".

When Miriam said this, she was silent, for it was to this point that the Savior spoke to her.

Andrew said to his brothers: "Say what you want to say but what you said, I at least, can't believe that it was the Savior who said it. Because certainly these teachings are strange ideas".

Peter added: "Did he really talk to you in private and not openly with us? Do we have to trust and listen to you all at once? He preferred you to us?"

He added: "Have you really spoken to you in private and not openly with us? Should we trust her and listen to her all at once? She preferred it to us?"

Then Miriam said to Peter, "My brother Peter, what are you imagining? Do you think that I thought of it myself in my heart or that I am telling lies about the Savior?"

Matthew answered and said to Peter, "You have always easily lost your temper, now I see you doubting Miriam as you would the adversaries. But if the Savior has made her worthy, who are you to reject her? Surely the Savior knows her very well.

"Rather, we should be ashamed of ourselves. We should become the Perfect Man, acquire him for ourselves as he commanded us, and announce the good news, without establishing any other rule or law that differs from what the Savior said."

"What should we do now?" James timidly asked.

Miriam turned to him, smiled at her Beloved's brother and said:

"What did he ask us to do?"

"To go into all the world..." John answered with determination.

She, who knew the Master's plan, simply said, "You will go east...and I will go west."

The disciples understood that her words were those of the Master.

Finally, Philip asked her:

"Did the Master give you a mission different from ours?"

They all looked at her in anticipation of her response. It was clear to them that there were so many things they didn't know.

She closed her eyes and placed her hand on her belly and let her mind return to those first days, three years earlier, when everything seemed magical and accessible.

Who was Miriam really?

***

Spring was in bloom. Fig trees offered a cozy shelter from the sun where rabbis often used to give their wisdom to their students.

Miriam walked along the little path leading toward the fig tree. He was sitting there when she spoked to him for the first time.

She had heard of this young rebel, the wonder of Galilee. For a long time, perhaps her whole life, she had been attracted by the mystery of God and interested in the news of the latest teacher and healer who would appear from the desert. Despite the vicissitudes and the many changes in her life, this was always her focal point.

Where was he? Was it really him? How would she recognize him?

She had never given in to the disappointment of false prophets, she felt that he would appear in her life and this certainty burned in her heart like a burning bush.

From early childhood, she perceived that she had a different way of perceiving reality from others. Not only because of her extreme sensitivity to all that aroused compassion but, above all, towards a parallel world that was invisible to others.

57

Miriam was modest about her resonance with the sacred dimension of the most ordinary things in life, but she also had a strong discomfort for the strong attraction she felt towards the male aspect, which highlighted her awareness of being born to find him. He would be infinite love and tangible flesh.

Her sister Martha was focused practical things and felt the burden of responsibility of having to protect her brother and sister from the things of life, and in her eyes, Miriam was an unconscious dreamer. Like all Israelis, she was waiting for the coming of the Messiah. She did not approve of Miriam expecting more than the nation's salvation and thought that her constant desire was self-centered. That longing had brought the sisters into all sorts of uncommon situations. Her brother Lazarus was less critical because it was inconceivable for him to analyze the behavior of his sisters as dictated by the culture of the time.

Miriam had listened to many rabbis, and often mixed with their disciples in order to hear them. One Saturday, she had heard men talking about this long-haired, piercing-eyed rabbi, who would be on the hills above the Jordan and would speak at sunset. Her heart leapt and she speeded up her pace to get home. She had to go and see for herself the one who was bringing a new message to the people from the day she heard the words echoing in the valley, "one greater than I is coming". The feeling that she would finally meet him was strong.

She must be beautiful like never before that day!

***

Miriam was the daughter of Cyrus, king of the tribe of Benjamin, and of Eucarestia. She had lived from birth in wealth and comfort, on the western shore of the Sea of Galilee, in the city of Magdala. It was clear to her parents from the beginning that their daughter had a special sensitivity and paranormal gifts. She had the small hazelnut eyes of an attentive child who studied people with the intensity and understanding of an adult and the guests who frequented her family often felt uncomfortable because Miriam seemed to know their thoughts and the depth of their souls better than they knew themselves.

As a child she often had dreams full of visions and a voice spoke to her about things considered by many Eternal Mysteries. The voice was familiar to her and she recognized when communications were unmistakable by trusting its words completely. She was guided by these experiences and comforted by them when the world around her became too cruel. At night it was not the city of Magdala, but another dimension that appeared to her that no one else seemed able to see. That dimension was populated by the souls of disembodied beings floating in the astral planes intrigued by her perceptive abilities and eager for compassion.

Miriam herself had tasted the expansion and peace that were there at higher levels because of an episode that put her life in danger. More than anything else, this event revealed to her that her identity was not limited to her body or her mind, but to a higher consciousness that revealed her timeless Self.

She loved to swim in the waters of the Sea of Galilee. Whenever she could, she left her family home and hurried to the nearby beaches, where she quickly got rid of her clothes and left them unattended on the shore. What she liked most was running into the water and then letting herself float on her back for a long time. She would looked up at the sky and lose herself in its infinite blue. She often closed her eyes and let herself be carried away by the water where the sound reminded her of the sweetness of a lullaby, making her feel like a child in its mother's arms. The relaxing movement of the gentle waves made her thoughts disappear. Her body completely relaxed in the warmth of the sun and, combined with the freshness of the water, it made her feel as if she was moving with the elements, joining the rhythm and peace of nature.

She could stay in that state for hours. She felt at home in that expansion that reconnected her, as if it were a return to a familiar state.

For her, this was one of the ways of joining with a vaster life. It was a kind of meditation and experience of quiet ecstasy. She did not know that the experience would lead her to an even deeper one.

This state was only interrupted when a frightening thought entered her mind, as when she wondered to what extent she had unwittingly drifted away from the shore, or when a distant boat sent waves toward her, or when any passing thought generated fear and uncertainty. Then she would suddenly start sinking. It was as if her floating on the water depended entirely on the tranquility of her mind, on her merging in faith and joy with the greater life that surrounded her. When a shadow of doubt entered the experience, she would lose her natural balance and integration with the world around her. This was a lesson she would never forget. It became fundamental to every circumstance. A positive, open and confident attitude kept her afloat, united to the current, connected to something greater. Any intrusion of the most fragile parts of herself, those with doubts and concerns, would upset this alignment with what Is, with God. From this experience, she learned to distance herself from the frightened ego that lived in the illusion of separateness, making her lose the feeling of being safe in the arms of the Mother. It was so clear to her that letting go and giving herself in full confidence to the wider life, the source of existence, was the only way to live fully.

One day, floating as usual in the waters of the great lake, she lost track of where she was and her head hit a rock that protruded from the waters. She lost consciousness. Her body continued to float for a moment, but it wasn't long before she was under the waves.

A fisherman standing on his boat while working on his nets witnessed the accident.

Miriam was quickly rescued and brought to shore. Her parents were by her side in minutes. Her brother and sister got down on their knees next to her, frantically trying to revive her. From that state, she noticed that her father was wearing his deep blue robe that she loved so much, and that he kept calling her. But her face was motionless and she didn't respond. She wondered, why? Her mother was in tears, praying aloud as she held her little hand. She seemed to hold her so tightly, but Miriam felt nothing. She could only look... from the top of the scene.

She clearly saw herself lying in the sand, her eyes closed. She could see the faces and movements of her family members around her. But she had no reaction. She felt as though she was floating in the sea, extremely peaceful. Only it was in the air, looking down on herself.

The liberation from the tension of emotions and fears was so great that it gave her a state of well-being she had never experienced before, and she realized that she never wanted to leave this place, this dimension of being.

It was the same reality she enjoyed while floating in the water, but much more extensive. The first experience was just a taste of this other one. Here was a feeling of belonging so strong that, without powerful motivation and effort, she did not want to go back. She loved with all her heart the people she saw beneath her. But she knew that her real home was here, in this other kingdom.

She wanted to continue to climb higher, moving away from the scene she was witnessing and fly towards the light.

At that moment, her father looked up and called on the God of Israel to save his daughter. She saw the tears in his eyes and his great despair and, at that moment, she wanted to return to herself.

She returned to her aching body and to her limits. Her body tremble, she coughed, and water came out of her mouth. She opened her eyes.

"I love you always, Abba," she said, and a great cry of joy resounded from all those around her. She had returned. Love had called her back despite the strong urge to go further in that other dimension that had opened up to her soul. This greater power of love was irresistible, stronger than her desire for light. She understood that she would sacrifice her eternal ecstasy to help others, to heal their pain.

As she watched those beloved faces covered in tears, she understood that she was bringing with her a new awareness.

With the passage of time and the routine of life she recovered by living in the richness of this double awareness.

How could her parents have believed her if she had tried to tell them that a presence unexpectedly manifested itself at night in her room, making her close her eyes tightly, while she felt its breath touching her ear and a light touch caressing her hair?

Or when in one of her many realistic dreams a figure of light manifested itself to dictate a prayer to her. Often, without explanation and with her heart in her throat, she was forced to ask her siblings Lazarus and Martha if she could take refuge in their beds in order to be able to fall asleep.

She never forgot their comfort, keeping forever a profound gratitude.

There was no one to explain to her why these supernatural events happened only to her in the family.

In her early years, these moments only aroused fears and tears and she had to quickly learn to manage them on her own and to live with them. This meant that little Miriam paid more attention to the weekly frequency with which her family went to the temple. The daily recitation of the Shema struck her deeply, resounding in her mind and heart with greater power as she grew older:

"Hear, O Israel, the Lord is our God, the Lord is One. Blessed is the name of His glorious kingdom for ever and ever. You shall love the Lord your God with all your heart and with all your soul and with all your might."

In that sacred atmosphere, surrounded by candles, the scent of incense and resins, songs and prayers, little Mira was one day raised to a state of ecstasy such as to make her feel floating a few inches from the ground. The ancient rituals resounded so strongly in her soul that it shook her heart with strong emotions, so much so that Saturdays truly became for her the sacred Sabbath, a moment of liberation and transmutation. The generation of these celestial feelings, of this spiritual expansion, connected her to a dimension of herself that was timeless, beyond this life.

She looked at the faces around her, the men with long beards listening attentively to the reading of the Torah and the women with their heads covered in expressions of deep and sincere devotion. She wondered if they too were raised beyond this earth as she was when she received wings of bliss that sent her to hover in an ocean of love that carried her straight into the very heart of God.

Mira would leave the Temple in concentration and, with these immense feelings, she would cling to her father's hand with all her strength to anchor herself to the earth, preventing her from floating towards the vast heavenly horizons. Her heart beat rapidly for a long time after service, leaving her breathless. No one seemed to realize what she had experienced and how shaken her soul was by the intensity of her encounter with the sacred. It became another special secret that she kept for herself and for which she wondered why. Sometimes she was confused but enthusiastic because she perceived that these incredible feelings created by the symbols, sounds and aromas of the temple were introducing her to a life she was destined to know, a life she had already known before. One day she would understand what all this meant.

Her unexpected experiences of another dimension confirmed to her the reality of the spiritual kingdom and of an existence beyond mortality, opening her heart and mind to the sacred teachings of her people. The sayings of the prophets, the imposing figure of Moses, the songs handed down from generation to generation from time immemorial, the holy atmosphere of the Synagogue.... All these influences that surrounded her entered deeply into her soul, becoming her reason for living.

Her faith was a certainty that matured in form through knowledge, and that familiar inner voice that she knew so well had never stopped pointing the way through her dreams.

As she grew older, she realized that those confused and difficult years had predisposed her to the perception of things to come. It wasn't long before her family and friends approached her for vision, advice, guidance.

Miriam was trying to be in tune with the other children of his age who could not know how hidden her childhood was, like the day Mira turned eight.

She was playing hide and seek with other children in the large garden of the family home. Trees, bushes, oriental plants were everywhere in this sought-after environment. The wealthy families of this desert land tried to recreate their version of the Garden of Eden through creative irrigation. In the middle of the garden was a circular labyrinth, a sign of their secret and esoteric devotion.

The children laughed and called out to each other. When it was Mira's turn to hide, she rushed through the foliage to find a good place where no one would find her. She knelt among the flowers and bushes and waited excitedly.

She listened to the other children who seemed far away. In that moment of silence, Mira heard other voices. She looked through the bushes to see where they came from.

She made her way, still hidden by the greenery, and saw through the leaves her two grandmothers sitting on a terrace talking.

"Have you seen with what joy our Mira is playing with her friends?" her maternal grandmother asked the other grandmother.

"Yes, even though I think she will always be a child," replied her paternal grandmother.

"Now it is time for her to learn what she needs to know....about herself, about her inner heritage and all that we need to pass on to her concerning ways to protect herself from negative energies...." her paternal grandmother said again, thinking of the importance of the moment.

"She is ready," replied the maternal grandmother.

Mira came out of the bushes and approached her beloved grandmothers.

"What am I ready for? "she asked.

The grandmothers smiled at her unexpected arrival.

"Your curiosity makes me realize that this is the right time," replied the maternal grandmother with a smile.

"There are things you need to know about our family and yourself," the other grandmother said.

"And on other worlds," added the maternal grandmother.

"And who told you that I don't already know anything about it?" Mira said to them, smiling.

"I don't doubt it," added her maternal grandmother, "Come closer, Miriam."

Mira crouched down in front of them and took their hands looking upwards from below.

"My love," said the maternal grandmother, "you're growing so fast... There's a time to play and a time to learn. Now is the time to learn."

"But the others are looking for me..." Mira replied.

"They may or may not find you. The important thing is that you find yourself," the paternal grandmother wisely said.

Mira smiled, "I'm here, Grandma!"

The Grandmothers loved her innocence and sweetness. Then her maternal grandmother leaned forward, moved her hair from her forehead, and looked deeply into her eyes.

"My beloved Mira," she said, "you must know that your soul is timeless. You lived before you were Miriam and you will live again, you have in you the wisdom of other lives and other worlds. You have returned to earth once again for a great mission."

Mira became serious and fully attentive.

"Remember this prayer that I will tell you now, because prayers have great power. Do not forget it and repeat it constantly."

She closed her eyes, preparing herself to welcome it into the depths of her heart.

Her maternal grandmother also closed her eyes and slowly recited the prayer in complete faith:

"The power of God envelops me, the might of God purifies me, and I am protected now and forever from everything and everyone: It's true!!!"

Mira opened her eyes and looked at her grandmother, smiling.

"I will never forget it, grandmother, I promise you!"

Her paternal grandmother said at that point:

"You are so precious, Mira, come closer."

Mira approached her other grandmother who put her hand on her head to bless her by saying:

"Grow holy and old, my daughter," she said solemnly, kissing her forehead. "Now go back and play with the others."

Mira smiled and left, walking through the garden with a reflective expression on her face. She touched the leaves, the flowers and everything that she passed by, seeing them in a new way. She found a ladybug on a leaf and gently caressed it with her finger tip.

Some of the other children appeared and rushed towards her. One of them said:

"Mira! We finally found you! Now it's your turn to find us."

Mira smiled, consenting with her head and resting against a tree. She covered her eyes with her arm and began to count. The children ran away to hide. After a brief moment, continuing to count, she headed towards the house.

She entered the big house and went through the rooms, looking for someone. She passed candles and Essene symbols on the walls, recognizing them for the first time. She found his mother putting cookies on a tray to offer to the children.

"Mamma..."

Her mother looked at her and smiled.

"Mira...You should stay outside and play with your friends. It's not time for a snack yet."

"I want to talk to you."

"About what, my little one?"

"The scroll hidden in your room."

Her mother interrupted what she was doing, aware that her little girl was about to cross the threshold of her innocence.

"Yes, the scroll!"

"I want to see it."

"Certainly," she said she smiling and putting down the tray. Mira ran into her arms, embracing her.

"Then it's time," her mother said as she crossed the room to pick up the precious box carved in mahogany wood, hidden and locked. She put it on the bed and opened it with a small key that she carried around her neck, threaded with a thin red cord. Mira sat by her side, eager to see what was in the box. With great care, her mother pulled out an old scroll protected by a sheet and proceeded to unroll it. Mira looked on with great interest.

"This is our family tree, Mira. Here are the names of all those from whom we are descended. Your ancestors," she said, indicating names and symbols on the scroll. "Your father comes from one of the oldest and noblest families of the tribe of Benjamin, going back to the days when our people were in Egypt. Our ancestors, the women of our family, were part of the court of Pharaoh. They were interpreters of dreams, healers and seers."

"Seers, what does that mean?"

"They are people who have the gift of seeing the invisible world, of being in contact with disembodied souls, of understanding dreams and predicting the future. From generation to generation, this gift has been passed down through the women of our family. It is in the blood, in the spirit. One of your ancestors was a beloved and trusted interpreter of dreams for the great pharaoh Akhenaten and his queen Nefertiti."

"Really? Mira exclaimed. "I know those names!"

"Of course you know them," replied her mother. "They are very important to our community. They have contributed to our Essene teachings and practices."

Mira was amazed and fascinated by everything that had been revealed to her...Her gaze was lost in the void, feeling that her awareness expanded to include the outside world and all its wonders. The sun was starting to set and she felt herself merge with the city of Magdala just as the purple sky slowly turned into a starry night. This was a day she would remember forever.

After a short time her maternal grandmother left her body.

One night, the moonlight poured into the large dark bedroom illuminating two beds in which a boy and a girl slept peacefully. In another bed on the opposite side of the room, Mira also slept. An oil lamp in the vicinity of the beds revealed the profile of their faces in its glow. An open book lay on the chest of the boy who was reading it before falling asleep.

The distant echo of a sweet and mysterious music resounded in the room. Mira awoke suddenly, her eyes wide open. It wasn't the first time and she knew what was going to happen, but she was always a little scared. The rustle of a light breeze shook the flame of the oil lamp which flashed for a moment and then suddenly went out. Mira closed her eyes so as not to see. She slowly slid under the sheets, leaving only the top of his head visible. She whispered the prayer her grandmother had taught her, keeping her eyes tightly shut: ""The power of God envelops me, the might of God purifies me, and I am protected now and forever from everything and everyone: It's true!!!"

She felt a presence sitting on the bed next to her.

Under the sheets, keeping her eyes closed, beads of sweat began to slide down her forehead, and she breathed deeply.

The book on the boy's chest closed by itself.

Mira felt her hair being moved to the side of her forehead, as if caressed by an invisible hand, and she recognized the familiar caress of her deceased grandmother.

The strange music enveloped her and Mira suddenly jumped out of her bed and hurried to one of the beds where the two other children slept.

She slipped in next to her brother who, despite being asleep, made her feel safe. She pulled the sheets up over her head and closed her large honey-colored eyes again.

Everything quieted down, Mira's breath slowed and she fell asleep.

One day her father had brought home a jewel bought from a passing merchant. The man had told him that it dated back to the time of the pyramids. Her father, a connoisseur of beautiful and authentic objects, had not missed the opportunity to buy it. He showed it to everyone in the family telling of the historical memory contained within it. He had placed it in a small chest, wrapped in a ruby red velvet cloth, on a table in the largest room of the house. The table was not high and little Miriam was fascinated and magically attracted by the jewel. One evening, while the family was busy in the other rooms, she wanted to hold it in her hands and place it on her heart.

Instantly, she felt a strong connection with it, as if its form awakened ancient memories buried in her subconscious. The amulet was made of turquoise paste and enamel, the size of an egg and in the shape of a scarab, so popular at the time of the Middle Kingdom and linked to the sun god Ra. It was said that just as the sun rolled every day across the sky, transforming bodies and souls, so the scarabs rolled their dung into balls to create a house where they laid their eggs and food for their newborn babies. They were seen as a symbol of the celestial cycle, of rebirth and regeneration. The Egyptian god Khepri, known as Ra at sunrise, was often depicted as a man with a scarab head. It was believed that this god renewed the sun every day before rolling it across the horizon to the other world, and then renewing it again. Queen Nefertiti was known to wear a golden scarab during her reign of the same size and placed against her heart.

These amulets were often put in tombs or hung on the neck of a mummy with a gold chain to protect the soul of the deceased from giving the wrong answers at the time of his final judgment.

Little Miriam's eyes filled with amazement and tears as she looked at the ancient amulet. She felt transported to another time, to another place. The sensation of being barefoot made her feel a warm paved floor under her feet, as if she were standing on a terrace overlooking desert sands warmed by the sun...She looked at her hands and recognized herself despite her complexion having the reflections of the cedars of Lebanon.

A warm breeze touched her cheeks as she leaned toward the talisman to look at the details. She was mesmerized by this living object to which she felt strongly attached. In her early years, she had spent hours observing the wonders of nature around her. Bees and ants fascinated her with their incessant and organized efforts to build the community. Now she was lost in this ancient amulet as if she remembered the ancient mysteries of another time, from which memories and tangible sensations emerged. Strange aromas from another place entered her nostrils and her consciousness, and the more she stared at the jewel, the more intensely these buried memories resurfaced within her. Her heart beat rapidly as she seemed to hear the sound of unknown notes coming from skillful fingers dancing on the strings of a lyre. Her mind was flooded with images and, for a moment, she was no longer in her father's house in Magdala, but in the Pharaoh's palace, overlooking the pyramids of Giza.

Despite the annual celebration of liberation from slavery at Hanukkah, her people had close relations with the land of Egypt. The old wounds were healed. Their cultures, and even their languages, had merged through centuries of interaction from trade and marriage. The most learned Rabbis of Magdala said that one of their beloved psalms was a mirror of the Egyptian Hymn to the Sun. The less rigid minds appreciated the wisdom of this ancient world where the Jewish people had found their own identity among the conquered tribes gathered to build the pyramids.

Egypt had given a welcoming home to one of Israel's religious communities. The chosen people were in constant conflict regarding their God and the sacred teachings handed down to them. Their priests had fragmented into different fields of opinion, but no one had ever separated from the current of Jewish society as did the mystical community known as the Essenes.

Born at the dawn of human history, they were thought to be the oldest of all the initiates, linked to the mysterious figure of Enoch, called by the Jews "the seventh from Adam" and "the man who walked with God". The name Esseni itself derived from the Egyptian word "kashai" which, among other meanings, meant secret. They were said to preserve the deepest wisdom of ancient Egypt, whose symbols of light and truth were represented in the word "chosen", which in the Greek world was known as "essen". This spiritual community considered itself the true "chosen people" and Miriam's family was part of them. They called themselves "Children of the Sun", which connected them directly to Pharaoh Akhenaten and his worship of the Aten, the sacred solar disk.

Miriam intuitively felt that the amulet before her eyes had been hers. She felt its presence which emanated from that object in front of her. The little girl felt that she was not looking at something on the table but at someone's eyes, someone she knew, someone she herself had been.

Fragments of images, sounds and aromas re-emerged from her soul, penetrating even her senses. She found herself in another place, as real as the reality of the room in Magdala where she stood. She heard the cheers of the crowd celebrating a royal presence, and intuitively knew that she was that person. Memories surfaced in her mind like a dream and came through her quickly, outlining her physical appearance in another life. It was as if a veil had been lifted and she could see herself before her birth in Magdala. She saw the sun shine on the multicolored gems which sparkled on the clothes she wore. She felt a strong presence at her side, that of a man who filled her heart with joy.

A feeling of power passed through her, as if the surrounding world were her own because that man had given it to her.

Then came another perception that seemed to be the very foundation of the first. An expansion of the soul without borders. She did not recognize herself only as a daughter of Israel named Miriam, but as a vast and unlimited spirit. This spirit was ageless, timeless, yet deeply rooted within her in the here and now, rich in memories.

Who was she really?

She was not just a young girl, daughter of the king of the tribe of Benjamin, or the empress of an ancient land, but an identity without borders.

Miriam no longer looked at the details of the world around her, even though she was still vaguely aware of the jewel she held against her heart. She felt transported to a realm of light, a realm that she recognized as her true home, from which she travelled through the centuries, to appear as one person then as another, while still remaining herself.

She was timeless and lived an eternal youth in mortal flesh.

How much time had she spent in this state? A few moments! But when she became aware again of her little body and the family table came back into focus, she knew that nothing would ever be the same again. She had glimpsed a dimension of herself that opened onto another universe of sensations, intuitions and awareness.

Returning from that infinite realm of light, she perceived that much of her fear of the unknown had vanished. She understood that she was not alone, that she had never been alone, that she was united in her boundless spirit with the reality that had always been with her.

"Mira..."

Her father's kind voice called her away from this wonderful moment. Immediately, she was just the little girl who had dared to touch her father's precious object.

"Open your hand and look at it, my sweet Mira."

Her father sat beside her, with a gentleness that exalted his bearded features. He was a tall and powerful man, radiant with authority, in the habit of expecting everyone around him to follow his orders. But with his little girl, he was an affectionate father who rejoiced in admiring her brilliant and curious mind. This strong man, who could silence a noisy crowd with his gaze alone, was now radiant with joy in front of his special daughter.

"Do you have any idea what you're holding?" he asked softly as he lifted her up to sit her on his lap.

Miriam looked into his eyes and said nothing. She could only be radiant with happiness for being in the arms of the one she loved more than anyone else.

"How could you have known?" her father continued, gently putting his hand on hers to hold the precious amulet together as if it were alive. Miriam couldn't get away from it. It was as if the object had magnetized her hands, just as it had done with her heart. Her father whispered, "I bought it for you, it's yours! "as he watched what was happening, understanding that Miriam had just had a profound encounter with this magical jewel of an ancient world that inexplicably belonged to her. He caressed her long, soft hair and for a long time they were united in a contemplative silence.

Miriam felt that her beloved Abba had sensed that a mysterious event had taken place in her soul. Trusting completely in his love and care, she gently opened her fingers that held the extraordinary talisman tightly. She knew that she had opened the doors to other dimensions within her and that they would never close again.

Mira looked at the amulet from different angles. Then she carefully observed the drawings carved on its back and belly. It was clearly a seal for an expert, rich in hieroglyphics. She studied them up close and retraced them with her finger. The extraordinary drawings seemed to come to life. She began to form words by moving her lips, as if she could give a sound to the images, as if she had always known them. But what came from her spontaneously were words in her own language. She was intuitively translating hieroglyphs.

Her father looked at her, amazed. His eyes opened wide as if he was witnessing a miracle. Mira spoke aloud, with a melodic timbre as in a song, the words emerging fluidly from an ancient memory:

Always loved by the Lord Horus

Horus, Lord always loved

Always loved by Isis and chosen by the Lord Ra

Horus, always loved by Ra

"How is this possible?" exclaimed her father. "I've been looking for a long time for someone to translate it."

Mira looked up at him, innocence and pure joy coming from her honey-colored eyes. It all seemed so natural to her.

"I finally found the best interpreter of ancient Egyptian writing. The words are exactly as you said them, my wonderful Mira! Exactly!!! You will never cease to amaze me!"

She smiled and they looked at the hieroglyphs together. The forms had impressed themselves in her memory, reappearing in this life with their meaning.

Horus... the hawk's head god of heaven, god of the Egyptians since the earliest times, related to the pharaohs, son of Isis and the resurrected Osiris.

Isis... the most significant goddess of Egyptian civilization, the devoted wife and mother and the most powerful sorceress in the universe because she was told the secret name of the supreme god. Isis, the first and last, the venerated and despised, the scandalous and magnificent, with her powers of healing and protection.

All these images of divinities and their mythical actions which represented the greater Truth, resonated in her soul in a very personal way. But more than that, they spoke directly to her as if they were a map of her inner spirit.

"Chosen by Ra...". These words resounded deeply in her soul from the very moment she said the name Ra, the sun god of Akhenaten and Nefertiti renamed Aten, who manifested the Unity at the heart of Creation, the life-giving energy that generated all beings. The Creative Force itself...the God of Abraham, Isaac and Jacob. "Chosen by Ra," as the Essenes had been called since time immemorial, the Chosen Ones, as her people had also been called, and as she felt in such an intimate and personal way.... She herself, chosen by Eternity for a yet unknown purpose... But what was known was the love that reached the core of her being and always surrounded her. She had a tangible sense of that divine love and never doubted it. She did not consider herself special...just particularly loved. And, in turn, she could love in a special way, having first-hand experience of the unconditional love of the Divine.

The hieroglyphics intuitively translated by little Mira opened the door for her to a new knowledge of how much she was loved. They spoke directly to her, like a cosmic message handed down across time from beyond to end up in her little hand.

Her father understood well the greatness of what he was witnessing. He knew that his daughter was blessed with the gifts of her bloodline and graces from higher realms. He had not yet realized that her inner being had surpassed anything he had ever experienced. He had known the great spiritual figures of the time, men and women shaped by an ancient and timeless wisdom and profound mystical experience. Getting to know these people had been the journey of his life. How could he have imagined that, in his child, he would find paranormal gifts greater than the masters of esoteric Egypt and the magi of the East, descendants of Zoroaster? He understood that Mira had been blessed with more than unusual powers. She had been prepared by Almighty God, in the course of her life, to manifest Him in a unique way, transforming the world unbeknownst to her. He knew that he would leave this world with a heart full of gratitude for participating in the creation of this person who was his daughter and a gift of the Divine. He felt privileged to have nourished her in her early years, while she learned to open her wings and become more than he could ever have imagined. He knew that when it was time to leave, his soul would be welcomed into celestial happiness for having done his most important work.

From that day on, things began to change for Miriam in a clear and radical way.

New gifts manifested themselves in her as if they had been generated by the memories of her previous existence. She discovered that she had the ability to intervene in events and bring physical and spiritual healing through her contagious joy. She realized this in an unexpected way. She was playing with her brother and sister when Lazarus climbed to the top of a long ladder, to show his agility. When he reached the last step, he jumped on the roof of the house that dominated the town, raising his arms in victory. The sisters watched him helplessly as he lost his balance. Helpless, they watched him fall backwards onto the bare ground. Miriam and Martha rushed to his side, panicked. He had fallen on his back and was bleeding from his arm.

"I can't move my legs," he shouted, terrified.

"I'll get help! I'm going to get mother!" exclaimed Martha.

Miriam, who had kneeled beside her brother, read the pain and fear in his eyes and felt the need to intervene, asking God with all her heart to be his instrument. She was afraid to touch him, for fear that his bones might be broken. He complained of pain, pleading with his eyes for her help. She had to do something for him while they waited for help. What could she do?

Suddenly, she began to sing softly. At first, she thought it was someone else's voice because she had not consciously chosen to do so. It simply came from the depths of her heart. She realized that she was singing the lullaby that her mother sometimes whispered when she held one of her children in her arms or when she sat at their bedside to help them fall asleep.

Miriam realized that her brother's fear was gradually disappearing. This encouraged her to sing louder and lose herself in the sweet melody. The more she sang, the more she witnessed a glow of peace and comfort shine through her brother's eyes. She continued to sing, and after a few moments, Lazarus tried to sit up. Miriam stood and took him by the hand to help him stand up.

Their mother appeared, running quickly toward them, followed by Martha and some neighbors.

"What happened?" Martha shouted, amazed at the sight of her brother standing next to Miriam, smiling.

One of the neighbors, the community doctor, told their mother not to embrace him.

"Wait! Look at his arm!"

The flesh was open, but it wasn't bleeding anymore. The doctor approached and examined the wound.

"This arm that was previously broken...is no longer broken! I know it's possible. But I have never seen it before," he exclaimed out loud.

"It was Miriam...," said Lazarus, staring at his sister with wonder and joy.

The adults looked at each other.

"I've heard of such a thing," said one of them in a serious tone. "There is a boy in Nazareth who is said to have healed some of the sick. I didn't believe it. But now...maybe these stories are true."

Hearing about the boy from Nazareth, Miriam immediately felt her heartbeat accelerate and the arrhythmia continued for a few hours. She listened intimately to what her body revealed to her and knew in a mysterious way that one day she would meet him and that this meeting which had been planned from the mists of time would change the course of her life. She knew these things with the same resonance that the ancient memories had generated in his soul. She knew that, however long it would take, it would be the perfect time to meet him, and she knew that she would recognize him.

Her family owned a house a few kilometers from the town of Nazareth. She remembered that she had been in this second house, but they had never gone to the village. She had to find a way to ask her father to take her there. Even though he loved to give her everything she wanted, this was a strange request and little Miriam would need a good reason to do so. Her character was such that she could not misrepresent the truth as her soul needed honesty and clarity like a man lost in the desert needs water. She was incapable of manipulation, even though she could see the weaknesses of others and, without effort, she could get everything she wanted from them. Her rare beauty only increased this power. But she refused to use it. Her natural humility and good heart ruled out any possibility of abusing her gifts to get what she wanted. Moreover, she wanted nothing more than peace in her heart. She had learned early on to follow the insights and inspirations that came to her from deep within. She knew that these spontaneous episodes were rooted in that voice she trusted with absolute abandon.

A few days later, she found the courage to approach her father with her request. He was in the meeting room where people came every day to visit him and ask him for his counsel. He had just finished advising an old man on his affairs as death was approaching. As the man asked for his blessing and left the room, Miriam approached her father. He smiled upon seeing her.

"Mira... I was about to come looking for you."

She approached the chair, and sat, as always, on his knees.

"You were going to look for me, but it's me who needs to talk to you."

"I have some news," said her father as he stroked her hair.

"Don't you want to know what I want to ask you?" she responded, eager to receive an answer.

Her father smiled at his daughter's impatience and with sweet authority said to her: "I want to tell you the news first, my Mira," kissing her gently on the forehead.

"We have to take a little trip."

A big smile spread on Miriam's face. She felt that destiny was coming to her. Already in these young years she had begun to recognize the synchronicity and interaction of events. Her hand tightened the amulet that her father had put around her neck and that she had hidden under her long white dress so that it would be in contact with her skin at the heart level.

Her father, at this final stage of the construction of their second home, had ordered his site manager to carefully supervise the details of the public meeting room at the entrance. He wanted it to reflect the craftsmanship and history of his people. The front room was to be designed to accommodate visitors from Capernaum and Tiberias who knew his reputation as a man of wisdom. It was less known that he was also a Grand Master among the Essenes and that this house in the heart of the Jewish countryside was to be a meeting place for all the brotherhood surrounding Mount Carmel, the heart of the Essene community in northern Israel.

Miriam's father imagined the symbols of their ancient teachings along the walls and ceiling of the new entrance hall that would be created by the best Essenian artists and craftsmen in the region. Among them was the carpenter of Nazareth, a humble and good man named Joseph.

***

A majestic sun rose above the small village known by history as Nazareth. But the day Miriam and her father made their journey, it had a different name: the place of the Nazarenes, because it was a community of Essenes gathered together to live their lives and beliefs openly but confidentially among others.

For most people a fisherman was simply a fisherman, it was assumed that he lived the ordinary life of a Jew, following the Holy Laws and respecting the customs of Israel. No one could suspect that this fisherman or carpenter was baptized every day at sunrise with the recitation of prayers written centuries before the Jews became a people.

In their common life, they remained hidden from the wrath of the Pharisees and Sadducees who despised the ancient and secret sect.

The Nazarenes were looking for purity above all in their way of life. For them, the Temple and its priests had become corrupt. A day would come when one of them would break the silence and call all the people of Israel to repentance and new baptism.

Their bond with Egypt would cause others to doubt their loyalty, especially in this time of revolt against the Romans and the call of their nation to return as they had been at the time of King David.

The law said that the Messiah would free the people from oppression. But in the city of the Nazarenes, it was known that another type of Messiah would appear. These ideas were too dangerous to be expressed in public.

From the balcony of their home, Miriam could see in the distance the profile of the town of the Nazarene. She watched the rays of the sun dancing on the flat roofs, glistening here and there as if they were reflected by objects along their trajectory. She felt those sparks in her soul, heart and stomach. She sensed that an immense event would happen because of this small town, but she could not identify it. She had the feeling that all this had been waiting for her since before her birth.

What did she expect? She had learned many profound teachings from her father. But in addition to what he taught her, she had confirmation of what she understood intuitively in her heart.

What she knew now, on the balcony, was that the meeting for which she had come to this town and this world was about to take place.

This was an event that would become her purpose and her destiny. All this she perceived in a mysterious way, intangible but so real. Instinctively, she held in her hands the ancient jewel hanging around her neck, a gesture that somehow seemed so familiar to her even though she had just begun to wear it. It was particularly significant to hold it in a moment like this - when the past, present and future met in a perfect alignment with the Eternal Here and Now in which perfect clarity manifested itself.

She realized that the amulet was warm in her hand. Was it the heat of her body that penetrated this relic of another time or was it a heat that emanated from the scarab? She wasn't sure. But what she sensed was that the amulet gave her a feeling of power, as if it revealed to the soul the nature of things to come. It seemed to generate in her the feeling of being in an ocean of light, an immensity that she could only identify as love, a love without limits, an exhilarating love, an ecstasy in which she lost herself... and at the same time she found herself for the first time.

She remembered when she had been on a boat with her father in the middle of the Sea of Galilee. The blue vastness calmed her soul, spreading a peace within her that extended to every part of her being. She felt as if her awareness had projected far beyond her body, running across the width of the water and rising to the sky beyond the clouds, making her head spin, as if she was losing her balance. It was a timeless feeling and she remembered that, for a moment, she was no longer the little Miriam, but a boundless spirit flying through infinity.

To stay standing she had to cling to the side of the boat. Her father thought at first that she had seasickness, but then he saw the light in her eyes and realized that his beloved daughter was face to face with the deepest reality of her being, with life itself, with her fusion with the Divine.

At that moment, the Sea of Galilee was only a drop in the great ocean from which the world had arisen. The connection she felt was now ablaze with the very revelation of the essence of life. That essence was Sacred Love rising like the sun through space.

On the balcony at her home, at this turning point of her existence, she perceived that this Sacred Love was the center of Creation and had to be witnessed through the incarnation of a human being who would reflect, as in a mirror, the reality that was also embodied in her.

The sound of the children playing near the house brought her back to "ordinary life". She found herself standing on the balcony, looking towards the children who had interrupted her extraordinary experience....... Or were they not interrupting her at all? Maybe they were part of this Unity.

Miriam decided to join the children. She loved the joyful energy of play and laughter, this celebration of life. But there was something else that attracted her to them. She felt that she needed to go down those stairs, and that she had to put her little feet on their own land and stay among them. That magnetic attraction in her solar plexus was unmistakable. The feeling was always the same: a quiet certainty of having to do it, even without knowing why. She trusted this inner impulse throughout her life. It was another aspect of the voice, though silent but with the same power.

She sought her father's permission to go to the courtyard. But she was unable to find him and chose to follow her desire to go down the stairs.

Going down the stairs, the rays of the sun entering through the open door grew with each step, until they filled her vision with their brilliance. When she reached the bottom of the stairs, all she could see was light. The happy sound of the children was heard outside. But in that cascade of light there was a sacredness that silenced her in amazement. She stopped for a moment, mesmerized by the golden light. Everything quieted down. Even the children's play seemed to fade away, like a distant echo. There was only that light in front of her, feeling like a living presence. In the shining rays, she thought she heard a subtle hum that seemed familiar to her.

Her eyes were still immersed in the brilliance of the sun when she saw a silhouette in the distance approaching, as if the light was creating a mirage. Miriam looking carefully, completely motionless.

There were two figures, that of a man holding a child by the hand.

Miriam's eyes saw through a gap in the light and the glow vanished like morning fog. Beyond the gate where the children were playing, a father and son were heading for the temple. Miriam felt the boy's gaze pass through her body and his eyes were the only thing she could see clearly. She could not look away from them along the entire stretch visible beyond the wall. It was a short time but it seemed infinite.

Their eyes focused on each other and she could see, incredibly, its unusual color, an iridescent alabaster containing the sky and the earth. He looked at her. His gaze was penetrating and very sweet, like a seal on her heart.

Miriam became breathless as she recognized something familiar in this boy, so different from other children. His soft features expressed a gentle nature, even if his eyes shone with an unknown and captivating power. She sensed that he was aware that she also knew something about him, something about them.

Were they memories? Were they premonitions?

Then the intensity of his gaze softened and a hint of a smile seemed to shine through his lips. That smile for Miriam was brighter than the sun that had filled her vision moments before.

His father spoke to him and the two of them walked away toward the city.

***

Many years had passed since that day but Miriam never forgot the color of those eyes.

Miriam reached the top of the hill, following the path on which she was walking, and saw him sitting with his back to her, under a tree. He was alone and seemed to be enveloped in a deep stillness.

There was no one else with him and she understood that the young rabbi was preparing to meet the crowd waiting for him impatiently and thirsting for truth.

Miriam had wanted to speak directly to him since she had stood behind a large crowd listening to his words echoing on the hill. The words he spoke that day had resonated deep within her soul as if she had said them herself. He had spoken as no one had ever dared before, with the authority and sweetness of those who knew the Father's will! His messages contained a power that elevated her beyond herself. but that at the same time seemed to root her in everything that existed. The words he used generated a vibration that could be perceived by any ready and open heart, and was reflected in the beauty and harmony of the surrounding nature.

This was a new way of expressing oneself, different from anyone that she had heard in the past. These were life-giving words, those of a great expanding soul, for people who had ears predisposed to listen in a deeper relationship with truth and with God.

Miriam knew that these were the words she had been searching for since the beginning of her conscious life. These were the words for which she had come into this life.

The man who spoke embodied these words in every gesture, in every look, in every breath. He seemed to be the very essence of what he said. No rabbi had ever made such an impression on her.

She stepped forward towards the fig tree, not knowing what she would ask of him, she just wanted to see his face, she just wanted to look into his eyes.

When she heard him days before, from her position in the back of the crowd, she had not been able to distinguish his features.

At every step, her heart was beating faster.

She felt that she was not only approaching this man but also something else, and she felt such a physical emotion that it manifested itself as an knot in her stomach. She sensed that this man was more than a master: he was a king. She was embarrassed by the intuition that he might be her other complementary half, but who else could say things so intimate and perfectly matching her perceptions? Who else could see the world and the Presence of God with an understanding similar to her own?

As she approached... he suddenly got up. His body stood with total grace, as if his consciousness was in every part of his being. It was a quick move yet rooted in the silence in which he had been immersed. It was as if he also knew that she was finally coming.

He turned slowly and his face appeared to her as though she were seeing him for the first time. Their eyes met and penetrated each other in a transcendental and vivid way.

She recognized the iridescent Alabaster..........!

Immediately, she felt a strange electricity flowing through her body. It was a once-in-a-lifetime experience, unique and transformative, almost separating her spirit from her body, while remaining completely anchored in the moment.

Her breath was trapped in her throat and time stopped.

Then that same soft smile on his lips appeared which was more than a thousand confirmations, all those she had been waiting for since they first met.

"So, it's you.......".

They looked at each other without saying anything, moments that seemed like an eternity.

"I am Miriam," she said in a whisper as his smile revealed his teeth, surrounded by the soft beard, which were of an unusual glow.

"I know...," Joshua said.

"We've met before in the city of the Nazarenes."

"Yes, there too..." were the only words he could say.

"I knew it was you," he said again, as the songs of the birds became silent.

"You knew it was me? What does that mean?" Miriam asked.

"This is the time we have been given."

"Time for what?" she said trembling

"For the great work..."

Miriam approached, took his hands in hers, unforgettably, and bowing her head kissed them.

It was a long kiss as if her soft lips wanted to leave their mark; he let her do it. Then she knelt down to kiss his feet. She had never seen such perfect feet, and approached them with reverence and modesty as her hair fell forward covering that gesture of intimate sacredness, while he stretched out his hand to help her gently rise.

As she stood up, she looked at him in astonishment, staring at the hand she had grasped and tightening her fingers around it. Then her gaze was lost in her eyes.

They were two big, deep eyes, filled with an expression of love that she had never seen before. There was an invitation in those eyes to let go, a magnetism that penetrated into the center of her being and seemed to say to her, "Welcome home".

Their faces were within a few inches of each other.

"All this was written," he said softly and with determination.

"Each of us is a reflection of the other, Two Aspects of the One."

Miriam listened and understood.

"We come from the One and return to the One. We are the One."

He knew that it was easy for her to absorb his words, even though she was so faithful to the teachings of her people, because she was an independent thinker.

"We are Him," he continued smiling at her. "He is in us... We are three in one."

Miriam immediately recognized the immensity of his words. She saw in the eye of her mind the triangles of the ancient Star of David with its cosmic meaning and the sacred geometry that was reflected there. She knew from her studies that the number three in the sacred numerology of her people represented the fulfillment of the divine work, the fulfillment of the Holy Will.

"We have come to the world in this time to accomplish a mission."

"What mission?" she asked, ready to give herself to him.

"To show the world our true identity and the path of return to the father. "

"I belong to you and therefore teach me the things I do not know to best serve God's plan..." she said in a trembling voice.

He looked at her in silence for a moment as if in an embrace. Then he spoke again:

"Miriam..."

Listening to her name at the sound of his voice seemed so familiar to her and yet she knew that she was listening to him for the first time. She recognized the very essence of herself in the way he said her name.

"Miriam," he said once again. "You are the path of return."

"Make me worthy, Master, at your side."

"I will follow paths that you will follow with me. I promise you. But one day you will carry your Cross like me, and we will go on until All is accomplished in this time."

"You are the Master", she said with deep devotion.

"And you are the Teaching," he replied with deep awareness.

She didn't seem to want to fully understand what he was saying. It was too much. This mystery was too great to be revealed before its time.

"As I told you, we are the same," he continued. "You will express me through your life."

She hadn't noticed that he was still holding her hand, and when she did, she held it tightly.

"I am..." Joshua said in a voice that reminded her of the vibration she had felt in the glow of the sun when they first met in the town of the Nazarene.

"I am..." she repeated.

He smiled a smile that dissolved her heart and soul, as if she were looking at the center of the Universe.

Then he spoke again:

"I am because you are... You have made me reborn. Without you, my mission cannot be accomplished. Without you, I cannot be complete. You are not just a part of me. You are me, separated in form from me for the good of this world."

"Now I know that I only love you..." persisted Miriam.

"There is nothing I am going to tell you that isn't already inside of you."

A tear slowly slid down her cheek. What her heart and ears had heard was the key to opening her Royal Door.

"Miriam," he said again softly, looking deep into her open soul, "you are the other half of my individuality, and I will show you this in time. All this is true now, in this eternal Now, and it has always been so".

He took her hands and pulled them to his lips, kissing them,

"Welcome, Miriam, My Bride."

From that moment on, they were inseparable.

***

Some of his followers often waited for him on the desert hillside where he retired after leaving the crowd, hoping to have the opportunity to talk to him in private.

They were anxiously awaiting him because his words that day stimulated them to ask him so many questions. They were ecstatic and motivated to wait for him! Some of them had given up everything to follow him. Peter had left his fishing business, which had been his family's tradition for generations. Andrew and Philip had left their teacher, Blessed John, for this former carpenter from a small town.

Why did those words resound in the depths of their souls as if they had already heard them before? Their beloved prophet John had said to them: "Behold the Lamb of God.....He must increase and I must decrease."

Their Master had sent them to him, a gesture that had never been made before among the followers of holy men. Everything was different now. There was a feeling that the world was going to be divided into two parts.

Slowly, many accepted all these new ways of thinking.

What struck them most were his reactions when he did not tolerate the hypocrisy of members of the religious orders. He faced these powerful men of knowledge and prestige with a firm will that no prophet before him had ever dared to implement. Not even the "desert-dweller" Amos who proclaimed the words of the Almighty on the rejection of their bloody sacrifices.

The young rabbi brought a paradox of infinite mercy and boundless courage that put them in awe.

But his greatest act of rebellion against the Holy Tradition and the expectations of the Jewish people was yet to come.

Joshua and Miriam walked close together, hand in hand, in the light of the day that was fading away, headed toward the men awaiting them.

Just as the sun disappeared, a golden glow rose from the horizon and formed a crown of light on their heads. As they approached his followers, Miriam gently withdrew her hand and let him walk a few steps ahead of her until he reached the camp fire they had lit.

Peter spoke for all of them and asked him:

"What do you mean when you say: Let the one who seeks continue to seek until he finds. When he finds, he will be disturbed. When he is disturbed, he will be amazed, and he will dominate over the All."

Joshua looked at the four seated men whose faces were illuminated by the fire and said softly:

"I mean that there is nothing that is not already in us, with us, to look for except within us, so when we find ourselves in front of ourselves and recognize that everything painful and wrong comes from our image reflected and deformed by the shadow of the ego, this will disturb us. But it will be enough to expose ourselves completely to the sun to save ourselves and others because each individual is part of the whole."

Miriam listened with deep attention as she sat in the shadows and the wood crackled in the flames. His words were so clear in their simplicity and immediacy, accessible to all intuitions from the most superficial to the deepest. She wondered if these men who listened to him were fully aware of what he had just told them. He had given them a key to liberation from the torments of life and an extraordinary hope that all might find their way to the light of true understanding. He had explained that it only takes the courage to see oneself as one believes oneself to be, and to strip oneself of deception in order to recover one's true nature. She was amazed by the promise of those words of light, by the certainty of being able to get out of our illusion to recover the fullness of life. How liberating it was to feel that the upheaval of the things of life came only from ourselves and that therefore we could free ourselves from that suffering.

"Tell us how our end will be," asked Thomas.

Miriam smiled, surprised that another question was already on their lips. Didn't they need some time to absorb the apparent simplicity of the last answer? They were ready because they were hungry for this knowledge, but didn't they need more time to contemplate these powerful and gigantic ideas so humbly expressed?

Joshua answered, looking into the fire, "Did you discover the beginning, then, that you are looking for the end? Because where there is a beginning, there will be an end. Blessed is he who takes his place at the beginning; he will know the end and will not experience death."

The silence that followed his words made it clear that this time they had difficulty understanding them, so he continued:

"Between the beginning and the end there exists the present that is eternal. Blessed is he who does not care about the end because he knows that being rooted in the awareness of his own eternity allows him to experience every moment of life in its cyclicality to which the word death is erroneously associated."

Miriam closed her eyes because she was overwhelmed by a feeling of satisfaction. "...of one's own eternity...". These words were a confirmation of what she had sensed for so long, and his reference to the cycles of life she had understood well from early childhood and from her ancient memories.

Knowing that some were deeply understanding him, Joshua continued:

"The father's reign is like a certain woman carrying a jar full of food. As she walked down the street, still far from home, the handle of the jar broke and the meal emptied behind her on the street. She hadn't realized it; she hadn't noticed any accident. When she arrived at her house, she put down the vase and found it empty."

They waited to hear his interpretation of this parable, the first to be pronounced.

"The kingdom of the Father is made of the fullness of the Nothing, our existence is a path of knowledge and unconsciousness to which we give the name of All. The dissolution of matter brings us back to the "emptiness-fullness" to which we give the name of God."

Miriam was deeply moved by this mysterious paradox. She felt in this polarity a perfect harmonic expression of the inexpressible which the mind cannot define.

"How do we approach God?" asked someone shyly.

Joshua said to his disciples, "Compare me to someone and tell me what I am like."

Simon Peter told him, "You are like an honest messenger."

Matthew said to him, "You are like a wise philosopher."

Thomas said to him, "Master, my mouth is totally incapable of expressing what you are like."

Joshua said, "I'm not your master. You drank, and you got drunk with the living water I offered you."

And he took Thomas with him, and said three things to him. When Thomas went back to his friends, they asked him, "What did Joshua say to you?"

Thomas said to them, "If I told you only one of the things he told me, you would collect stones and stone me, and fire would come out of the rocks and devour you."

They asked Thomas again what his words had been in private.

They were ready for anything to get to the truth, and they insisted on knowing these revelations.

Thomas repeated his words: "All that is visible and all that is invisible is a manifestation of the Logos or Heavenly Father, like me, like you and like wine that has clouded your mind to make you lose all inhibition and prepare you to know the great truth: I am God... but you are God also. You will discover this only when you are worthy!"

"How do we become worthy?" asked Peter.

Joshua said, "What you have will save you if you make it emerge from yourself. What you don't have in you will kill you if you don't have in you."

Then he went on to be more explicit by saying:

"Within every man there is the potential to escape from the prison of his own deception, and only when he has made his essence clear is he granted the antidote."

"Who is this to give us such words?" Matthew wondered, amazed by what he was hearing.

"When you undress shamelessly, take your clothes and put them under your feet like small children and trample on them, then you will see the son of the living, and you will not be afraid."

"What does this mean?" Peter asked with a certain agitation, trying to understand well what the teacher was saying.

"To strip yourself of your own roles and beliefs requires a great act of courage and humiliation, but you will see that this will make you return to a state of joyful childhood. Only then will you be able to look in the mirror and discover that you and I are one."

They all sat in silence for a long time. The fire was extinguishing and the cool desert breeze surrounded them. Miriam looked at the faces staring at the flames. She realized the vital need for these men to know the deeper things in life, but she also thought about their earthly needs. They hadn't eaten since before the Master had spoken to the crowd and it was starting to get cold. This brought her back to her maternal essence.

In the generous spirit that characterized her, Miriam understood that they had no place to eat and no place to stay. She got up and thought of inviting them to her home, knowing that Martha would gladly cook for them. Both she and her brother Lazarus had heard of Joshua and were deeply moved by his teaching. It would be an honor to host him and his followers.

He also stood up and turned to Miriam and smiled, knowing what she was going to say. This was one of the many times that he anticipated Miriam's words before she spoke, proving himself capable of reading thoughts before they were expressed.

***

Martha had not asked any questions when they arrived, recognizing Joshua and his friends, and was pleased that Miriam was so integrated into the group and so close to him. She immediately understood what was happening between her sister and Joshua and naturally felt that her role would be equally important, though practical, and began to take care of the four men who ate her food with appreciation and gratitude. Lazarus added a chair to the table. He was a quiet man but to make them feel more comfortable he sat down to eat with them. He felt inexplicably happy to host them and was heartened to know with whom Miriam spent her days. They were men who had to work hard from early youth and came from a reality that generally had little time or energy to devote to spiritual matters while Lazarus had the privilege of studying and traveling to discover other cultures. He recognized that these men had left everything behind to know God more closely, while he had stayed home to study ancient philosophy.

His aspiration for the Essenes kept him focused on their community and rituals, preferring this quiet life to body fatigue.

He observed them with respect, thinking that these men were an example of the backbone of the towns in which they lived. Their sweat and work made possible the daily existence of everyone else. Now they were vagrants, a brave choice, following this new rabbi who called them to a kind of life based on awareness and devotion.

Lazarus had wondered in the past why a young and promising man like Joshua had left the life of the Essenes to wander in the countryside of Galilee. Looking at these men, with their faces marked by wind and their hands made knotty from labor, he realized that Joshua was leading everyone toward true spiritual life, regardless of class or education. He was tearing down the walls separating the social classes and introducing a new connection in which all were equal, all were part of one body.

Discovering that his sister Miriam had joined him made him realize that the message he was carrying was different, important, filled with a transforming power never seen before. He knew that Miriam was very perceptive and independent of all the ideas circulating in the nation. If she had chosen him as her path, then it meant speaking in a new language that transcended those of the past. He knew that his sister had searched long and hard for something she could never define and often told him that she would only recognize him when

117

she listened to her heart. He trusted her inner resonance, her purity of mind, and accepted confidently that from this small beginning a great event would emerge.

Miriam and Joshua were on the terrace overlooking the city of Bethany, sitting quietly in the flickering light from candles that softened the darkness of the night.

Miriam had brought with her in a pocket of her long, wide skirt, a small alabaster vial filled with a precious oil that she herself had created. Her love of nature was such that she had learned the secrets of plants from which remedies and perfumes could be extracted. She had dedicated years to herbalism, finding in the creation of new aromas a direct channel to her own essence.

She opened the bottle and a sweet and intoxicating scent of musk and sandalwood was released into the air. This was her favorite perfume, containing drops of myrrh and lavender wisely dosed. The aroma reminded her of the large trees in the forests of Gaul where she had traveled with her father when he bought spices from Western merchants in the shadow of the majestic oaks where the druids went to collect their sacred plants. That is why she preferred it to other oils, it was perfect for her husband, the man sitting next to her: strong, deeply rooted, with a hypnotizing radiance. She recalled the saying of the prophet Isaiah: "They shall be called oaks of righteousness, a plantation of the Lord for the display of his splendor". She had listened to these words every year since childhood, and they had always resounded in her with a special quality. Now, sitting next to her man and Master, she knew from the beginning that the one who spoke to her was the one who would enter the eternity of her cells. The words that echoed in her mind were those he had read at the start of his ministry in the temple of his hometown: "The Spirit of the Lord is upon me because he has anointed me......." They had lifted her into endless moments of ecstasy.

She took a linen towel and placed it on her lap, kneeling before him.

Then she took an empty pewter bowl that was under the table and slid it next to her. Gently, with her eyes fixed in his eyes and without saying a word, she took his foot in her hands, poured water from a pitcher, and washed his feet. He looked at her in silence, enraptured by her sweetness.

After removing the dust of the desert from his magnificent feet, she dried them with the soft linen, poured a few drops of the perfumed oil she had in her hands, and massaged his skin carefully with her magical, loving fingers covered with the royal aroma.

When Miriam was finished, he said to her in a deep voice: "Have patience and faith and let me guide your hand...give me time to gather the ripe ears of wheat in the heat of your blinding light of love."

She looked at him with her hands still covered in oil. Her eyes expressed all the unconditional desire of her state. She belonged to him completely.

He continued:

"Nothing and no one will gather our intentions if they are not as clear as spring water."

She nodded. Her whole life had been built on the cornerstone of purity. She knew that there was nothing more important than those foundations.

"Are you ready for what is about to come?" he asked with masterful sacredness.

"I've always been ready...even without knowing what exactly I was looking for," she replied.

"So much will be asked of us...." he said softly.

Miriam whispered:

"In mutual exclusivity and purity of purpose we can do anything."

He smiled with a smile that illuminated her soul like the rising sun.

"Yes, together we can do everything because we wish it...", he said. "But know that without you, I could not. Without you, my life would remain incomplete."

She stood up, her long mahogany hair covered her face for a moment and she sat down at the table next to him.

"Miriam..." he continued. "It was written that we would be together before we were born in this form."

"Everything that came before our current meeting," she said as her heart was beating faster, "prepared me for this moment."

"This is the turning point in human history. But how it will develop after us, after we have completed our mission...This will remain uncertain. You will be the one who will have to guard our fire to project it into the future, so that from our union the right fruit may be born from the tree of life...".

"Will people recognize and accept what is given them?" she asked without shame and with a timeless childlikeness.

"There will always be confusion in the world," he replied. "But he who truly seeks the Light will find it."

"Why should it be like this?"

"People must want what is offered to them with all their heart...".

"Why do they reject it?"

"Because life itself is... the only way home."

Joshua looked across the terrace at the soft light that outlined the horizon and beyond. The dark landscape was illuminated by the light of the moon.

"The illusion is so strong...that the need to survive makes us rooted in this world despite our stellar origins."

He looked up at the stars again, dwelling on Sirius, which shone in the sky like a pure diamond amidst so much sparkle.

"I sensed it from childhood", Miriam said, "that I was more than anyone in this life told me I was... this made me feel different from others".

Joshua, who held her hands, noticed that they were trembling and brought them to his mouth, kissing them. The kiss was so warm that she felt the heat expanding from his lips and spreading throughout her body.

"Miriam...you are much more than you can imagine. We come from the Light, the place where the Light was born from itself".

She looked into his eyes and felt as if she was looking into the infinite.

"But we are also mortals... Why?"

He replied, "Certainly, the flesh will age and disappear. And even if we express ourselves through the flesh and are known by it, we are beyond the flesh. You do not yet know your power, but you will know it only when the fire will burn your limits."

They looked at each other in silence. Then he uttered words she would never forget:

"Miriam, you will be the only bride for whom I have been true and eternal, the only hope to be able to continue to live in the cells of creatures who will know unconditional love."

A new understanding arose in her soul and tears of unspeakable joy made her eyes sparkling like stars. She realized that he was revealing something immensely high and transcendent to her, that the very reality of cellular tissue would change forever.

***

Miriam returned to herself in the small room by the green door, with her hand on her belly. Was it the contact with the tiny life that was beginning to palpitate within her that gave off an unusual warmth? She opened her eyes and felt like she was emerging from a dream. It seemed to her that she had been away from this little room for a long time. The sun was fading, but it was still daylight. Her most intimate memories had come to her in a flash, bringing her instantly through a review of her lifetime and the events that had brought her to this moment.

She was aware that the disciples were waiting for her outside, to share their last greetings before each of them headed down their own path. But the clarity of these memories had raised her above the moment to see the full panorama of her existence.

She realized that she was the center of everything. She realized that putting her hand on her belly was a gesture to seal the holy wedding that had opened the doors of her journey to eternity and at the same time brought her here for this purpose.

Her eyes rested on the chalice on the table in front of her. The simple cup that had been passed from hand to hand, in the symbolic sharing of his blood carried with it the experience of that last night.

This chalice had been part of their daily life before it was used for such a sacred sharing.

She took it in her hands. Immediately, it released a magical aroma of must and cinnamon of the kosher wine that it had often contained, awakening past scenes and ecstatic feelings of passion.

***

It was the second year of her time with him and his brothers chosen to bring truth to the world. His fame had grown rapidly. Tales of his miraculous healings and exorcisms had crossed the nation. Jerusalem also knew of this great holy man: had Elijah returned to them again?

The excitement and frenzy spread from city to city and the group of disciples grew with an enthusiasm that was reaching new frontiers.

Who was he really?

Only for Miriam, it was more than all of this! He was the man she loved beyond all limits, the one with whom she had found a unity of soul, spirit and body by opening the doors to her True Self.

In their growing love, one transformation after another took place in her heart and soul, becoming more and more who she had always been.

Miriam knew that the greatest miracle was unknown to everyone around him. It was the hidden miracle of their great love, and of their total fusion that made them One.

How quickly they had recognized in each other the exact half of the other. How quickly the ecstasy of their passion had generated a parallel and secret life, in which thoughts and feelings were unanimous and shared in perfect harmony. How much new joy had been generated by them for the good of humanity! Her heart was constantly expanding and Miriam was filled with such an abundance of feeling that it was essential to give herself completely and take care of the one from whom all this infinite good had sprung.

This infinite explosion of unconditional love made the rest of creation more vivid, transforming everything into a new sun shining from the fusion of their souls. For the first time, she understood in a tangible way how important the human being was for the manifestation of the Divine on Earth. Despite its apparent fragility, man's flesh and blood were also the transmission of the holy, not only for its reproduction, but above all for its incarnation. The sacred could be seen in what seemed most vulnerable. Even those who lived in darkness and in the repression of their real nature of origin drew from this union the vivid mirror of what they were supposed to be.

Everything became miraculous for Miriam, from the most natural expression of the divine compassion that emanated from Joshua, to the most ordinary sharing of bread at a stranger's house or on a Galilean hillside.

Miriam's ability to love, awakened in her a cosmic dimension, and gave her a contagious splendor. She would bring protection, healing and redemption, even with a single smile. Her infinite freedom of mind rose to ever new heights on the wings of this sacred love which passed through her eyes, her touch and her words to reclaim itself. She lived the moment in a full and complete way, in perfect harmony with the presence of the Eternal One, and others could feel her renewing power just by being in her presence.

When they were in silence, the goodness and purity that emerged from her made her fly to heaven with every breath she took.

It was the very purpose of life, the great conscious life that seemed to finally manifest itself. Each event was a message, a sign, a communication. Throughout her life to come, her colors, her creations, her inspirations and her circumstances became a language of love through which Life revealed her secrets and her protection.

The sacred was present in physical form because the key that had unlocked this consciousness was her purity and total devotion.

Memories returned to flow through Miriam's mind.

Joshua was on the boat on the waters of Galilee to speak to a large crowd gathered on the shore. His disciples who were sitting next to him helped anchor the boat, while others assisted the crowd.

As always, Miriam sat aside, but her presence was felt as if she were a part of him. They were always together, even if physically distant. He was the teacher, she was the inspiration. They shared every decision, every step, every experience, every look. For those around them, they were a manifestation of a unity that had never been seen before. She was his thoughts, he was her voice. Their lives were one. There was no longer one without the other. This was the example to imitate, the union between the finite and the infinite, like an ever-burning bush. It had to be witnessed because this was the meaning and ultimate purpose of the man and his woman, of the union between opposites, through the body to reach the soul and the divine spirit. They were the visible manifestation of the New Ark of the Covenant.

Miriam knew what Joshua would say to the crowd. He had explained to her that his sermons arose from the conversations he had witnessed as a child and from the questions he had asked himself since then and answered in the course of his physical and inner maturity. Miriam had suggested that he use the ancient practice of parables to convey his teachings as if he were in a crowd of children. She had appreciated this method of expression among the Essenes who gathered at her home to discuss it with her father. It was a practice that went back to the dawn of the Jewish people and their roots in other cultures.... She realized that images and metaphors were able to convey to each mind its own meaning, exactly what everyone was able to receive. It was a universal and timeless language that transcended all cultures and philosophies because it went straight to the heart.

Joshua's studies had introduced him to the profound thinking of the scholars of the Essenes and the enlightened ones of India and Tibet. He had traveled far and been away so long that he had changed radically just as his language had changed, and he had to find a formula to talk simply to the ordinary people of Judaea.

Although Miriam was well educated and raised in the home of an Essene Grand Master, she had remained in close contact with the people of humble extraction. She was loved by all for her respectful and spontaneous ways and for her jovial spirit. Despite her position in life, others were equal in her eyes, they were one caste: humanity! Her sometimes childlike carefreeness and joyful laughter put everyone at ease. Even in her most intense moments of discussing the deepest issues of the sacred, her positive energy and reassuring demeanor was contagious and made everyone receptive to greater understanding.

Joshua had an intense physical and energetic presence. He often intimidated both high-ranking officials and priests, as well as ordinary people. He was kind but serious, and although he could laugh and participate in everyday life, he did not behave with the lightness and sweetness that were part of Miriam's nature.

She was always ready to enjoy life, singing and dancing, ready to play with children and animals sharing her joy. He was mainly introspective and contemplative, always carrying within himself a deep peace, which for some seemed otherworldly and sometimes even disconcerting.

Miriam soon understood that his presence balanced his clear masculine polarity with her feminine polarity. In this way, the divine manifested itself through the respective roles assigned to them in form to proliferate unconditional love.

The people had many expectations, were in devout awe of Joshua, and loved the discreet presence of Miriam. Often, after he had spoken and retired into meditation, the closest followers gathered around her to ask her more precise questions and listened to her explanation and her way of expressing the same thoughts.

He often spoke of perseverance as a central effort to live a deeper life. He spoke of the need for vigilance and attention in order to remain on the narrow path of God's remembrance.

Those who had remained passive in listening to his words and returned home to live their lives in the same old way were responsible for the consequences of their choices. Those who needed a greater light to understand what they were learning found comfort in Miriam. She was always smiling, generously available and attentive to all their needs.

One day, after Joshua had spoken to the crowd, many had been disturbed by what they heard and some of the disciples tried to approach Miriam. A number of followers had left the group that day in response to what Joshua had said but some absolutely wanted to understand what he really meant with those parables.

They were walking along the path that led to the house where they had been sleeping for a few nights. Joshua had climbed the hill to gather in prayer and meditation, feeling the need to be alone with his heavenly father after a day of miraculous events. John was the first to speak:

"Miriam, please explain to us what Joshua meant when he said, "You don't look for me because you saw the signs, but because you ate those loaves and you are satisfied."

Miriam, concerned about their inability to understand and taken by compassion for their anguish and their uncertainty, said:

"Joshua refers to the fact that our lives have been numerous and with them our parallel evolution has acquired the consciousness of God."

"He told us to get the food that does not die," said Matthew with a worried expression on his face. "And that the Father has put his seal on him."

"The food that nourishes us forever," Miriam replied, "is the one that satisfies the soul with the awareness of our true inheritance and that we pass down from life to life only through unconditional love. This is the seal."

Philip came forward beside her: "People want to know what do we have to do to make God's works work? What can you tell us Miriam?"

Miriam answered without hesitation:

"To understand and recognize in every thought, word and action when our true essence is not expressed, our SELF, but the I AM which, deformed by the shadow, becomes EGO and is brought back to light."

Everyone reflected on the depths of his words. Then John spoke again:

"He said that the work of God is to believe in him whom He sent".

Miriam smiled, recalling the sweetness of his voice at that moment.

"Faith is a grace and when man does not possess it he must investigate until he finds it by surrendering himself completely to the will of his heavenly Father, only then will he float in an ocean of peace."

Nathanael had joined them as they proceeded down the hill and listened carefully.

He asked her what sign he would make so that they could recognize him and believe in him.

She turned to him and saw a confused look in his eyes.

"Truth is expressed through the coherence between word, thought and action. This state makes it possible to resonate with the divine in every manifestation, and everything becomes possible and miraculous because it is harmonious."

John was moved by her response. His quick mind brought him back to all the teachings he had studied.

"Our fathers ate their manna in the desert. He says, He gave them bread from heaven to eat."

Miriam stopped in front of an old olive tree on the side of the road. She picked up a twig covered in small leaves, which would serve as crumbs and, with resin and incense, would be used to bless the next house that would host them with their fragrant smoke, as was the tradition.

"Heaven and earth are the same thing, as above so below. When our mind burns the ignorance of thought in the sun of knowledge and becomes like the scented reverberation of the desert, it receives nourishment from the breath itself."

John intervened, "But Joshua said that Moses did not give our ancestors bread from heaven, that it is the Father who gives bread from heaven, the true bread."

Miriam, who had stopped for a moment to listen to him, continued to walk along the path, holding the twig of olives between her fingers and offering a few leaves to her friends.

"Moses knew the laws," she said, "because he had accomplished the great work of transformation, and everyone has access to true nourishment through the process of transmutation."

"What did the Master mean when he said that God's bread is the one who comes down from heaven and gives life to the world?" John asked again.

"The bread of God is the man himself who consciously generates himself to know himself," replied Miriam.

Nathanael hastened his pace and moved in front of them. He turned again to Miriam, hindering the path, revealing his inner conflict.

"But Joshua said that *He* is the bread of life...that those who come to Him will not be hungry."

"And those who believe in him will no longer be thirsty," added Matthew.

135

Miriam was still in the middle of the path. Everyone gathered around her, knowing how important her response would be. She spoke slowly and emphatically.

"He came to tell us the truth about our identity. Now it's all up to us."

There was silence as they absorbed her words. Then Philip walked nervously, thinking about the events of the day. He turned around quickly and said:

"But so many don't believe it. Look how many friends have left us!"

"This is the limit of their biological process, it happens when you are not aligned with the intelligence of the spirit," Miriam declared and in a reassuring tone added: "He will not reject anyone. He once said to me, 'I am your reflection, everything that is reflected in me becomes me.'"

Seeing that it was difficult for them to understand, she continued:

"Although he was born with the consciousness of the Self, he wanted to show us the path he had taken before us to pave the way and to get us out of the labyrinth of the mind."

In this moment of quiet contemplation, Miriam knew that it was the right time to give them more understanding as it had been a day of trials and contradictions for them.

"Anyone who has persevered in faith and practiced good with thought, word and action, elevates his spirit and then discovers that he was never born and therefore never destroyed."

Philip was stunned.

"But he said to the people before the priests, 'I am the bread that came down from heaven'."

"Yes, he did," Miriam answered gently. "He embodies the words that nourish the truth."

"Those who came from his town no longer wanted to listen to him, because they know his mother and father. How could he make such a statement?" Philip exclaimed.

"Matter in all its forms is a manifestation of the same substance as the father," Miriam stated, knowing that it would be difficult to understand. Then she added, trying to encourage them: "Truth that fears nothing and no one is the only law that saves."

Philip continued with a broken voice:

"He said to everyone, "I am the bread of life."

Miriam approached him, and placed her hand on his forearm, calming him with her presence.

"He was saying: I am what you truly are, and if you feed on my teachings and cultivate them, you will be like me, eternally alive.

He who has not cultivated and persevered in the purity of the spirit," she continued, "after realizing the truth and believing himself to be privileged and powerful, will give satisfaction only to the body and then die. The bread that comes down from heaven is consistency."

Nathanael could no longer hold back what tormented him most:

"Joshua said, 'If a man eats of this bread, he will live forever and the bread I will give is my flesh for the life of the world.'"

Miriam knew that this was the greatest concern for all of them, that these words had driven out the other followers.

"He is made of flesh and bone like all of us, but he is embodied in this body with the intention of helping humanity to make a great global evolutionary leap by freeing us from the fear of pain and death."

They were almost at their destination so they slowed down the pace trying to learn more.

Miriam concluded by saying:

"Eating and drinking his flesh is a metaphor for his sacrifice in having returned to this body out of love for us and we should never forget it. He showed us the way and the courage that we should all have in seeking the truth at all costs, having the certainty of life beyond the limit of the flesh and impressing this experience on the biological memory on earth for those who will come after us."

Now everyone walked in silence, each with a new understanding of what the Master had said. Miriam had freed them from their uncertainties. It was a new step upwards.

When Joshua went out to climb the desert mountains to pray, her house was open to support those hungry for understanding and mercy. That mercy was made known by Joshua and testified to by Miriam.

Their different ways of speaking merged into a single revealing expression of the great mystery. Joshua's words contained the power of thunder, Miriam's words consoled the spirit. He called people to great efforts and actions, she raised them up by showing them the easy way of faith and abandonment with the attitude of a mother. When He punished religious leaders, she understood their limitations. Both spoke little of divine judgment, but rather of forgiveness. Dying to oneself to awaken to oneself was the meaning of the whole process of rebirth. During Joshua's public appearances Miriam's natural shyness took over and she preferred to listen to him from afar. But sometimes small groups of people asked her questions, and she opened like a flower in the sunlight and enchanted the listener with a combination of joy and knowledge, expressing all her ecstatic knowledge.

Her eyes perceived the essence of the souls in front of her, and like Joshua did when his gaze penetrated her and she abandoned herself, they also let themselves be investigated. Joshua's presence electrified the atmosphere and, combined with Miriam's presence, soothed it.

Together, they made possible the tangible presence of the divine as never seen before and this perfect harmony between opposites was the reflection of the Truth for the creation of a new being: The New Man!

What was this new man, this new creation? Was it what Miriam had studied so intensively to find the path to a new kind of enlightenment, which transcended knowledge and was completely rooted in love for the divine? Her yearning for this understanding had caused her much suffering. Of course, she had been blessed with beauty and riches, but none of this satisfied her except for the need to immerse herself completely in God's consciousness. People had acted against her, trying to make her vulnerable in order to possess her or to take advantage of her generosity. She could never be sure that there were no ulterior motives in the attention and affection of those who declared themselves friends or lovers.

The carnal attraction she generated had long since lost interest in her. It was absolutely not flattering to be seen only as an object of desire by wise men veiled behind apparently impeccable social or spiritual behavior. She had come to accept the limit that most men revealed to her when captivated by her beauty.

Why were they all so predictable whatever their extraction, whether they came from the most noble families or the most common workers? Only a few more reflective people recognized that in front of them was more than a woman of great inner beauty. Her natural wisdom and predisposition to generosity made her attractive to even the most reflective, along with her physical appearance.

Very few were really interested in trying to see into the depths of her being and to recognize the origin of another type of beauty, that of the soul. It was this quality of her being that forged such a fascinating combination of soul and body, combined with the characteristics inherited from her ancestors of different ethnicities. In the various expressions of her being,

141

her energy produced a vibration in which there was a tonality that came from a nameless, inexpressible quality.

There was a strong feeling of being in front of an old soul, but it was more than that because it was a kind of quality that was born from a deep suffering of the acceptance of events coming from the will of God. A suffering that had been endured, faced and transcended. What remained to be understood by those who could, were not scars or unhealed wounds, but a new type of knowledge, a power of empathy and compassion known only to those who would walk in the valley of tears, in the shadow of death, in the desert, accepting the sacrifice of themselves for a greater love: humanity.

It was this deepening of the soul that could be felt, even if it was utterly inexpressible. It was this testimony imprinted in her eyes that few perceived, and only the most sensitive read what pains they had seen ... and overcome.

Many women, some very close to her, had been terribly jealous of her. Almost maniacally. Although by her very nature she was absolutely faithful, the fear that her beauty would drive their men away from them was dominant. Beyond that, there was indignation at how blessed she was, as if she were particularly loved by God. Her childish innocence and purity meant that those who did not have such qualities mocked. How dare she be who she was? How dare she be so beautiful and rich? How dare she love God so much?

Throughout her life, these feelings of anger and envy had arisen in unexpected circumstances even from good people. Her extreme sensitivity was able to perceive all these unspoken emotions by exposing those who blamed her and made them involuntarily aggressive. This had deeply disappointed her because she had never been guilty of any of the fears that others had about her. Her only desire was to do the right thing, the good thing, towards others, helping them to find the rot in their souls to be able to get rid of it. But often their egos and jealousy were too entrenched to eradicate them only with her innocent and loving intervention, and she began to leave them to her own destiny without interfering anymore.

This led her to choose not to surround herself with unevolved people, preferring more and more to be alone. She had never been lucky to find a good friend with whom to simply share her existence, without falling into these dark reactions, even with her sister Martha. Especially after the death of her beloved father, she had to learn to defend herself against everything and everyone.

No one could have imagined that Miriam had experienced such inner pain. No one could have imagined that this happy and carefree woman had wept all the tears that her body was able to shed, and that all that remained of those tears caused her eyes to burn with great pain. She never spoke of these things as her private pain could only be shared with God in an unconditional love so great that the past itself was healed from its light and the knowledge that she was so fully loved, recognizing it in every event.

This fusion with God was the salvation of the heart, soul and body. This was the totality, completion, meaning and purpose of her existence. This was the very heart of God and she had recognized it only in the eyes of Joshua, the love she now shared with the one for whom she was born. Finally, she had found it with this new creation that would take humanity to a new evolutionary level.

***

Miriam had held the cup in her hands during these memories. How short had their time been together, and yet how full!

Her mind returned to the present. The room was becoming darker as the sun tilted toward sunset, beneath the window. She heard the whispers of the disciples outside the open door. It was time to say goodbye... forever. She knew they would never see each other again. She knew the kind of transformation they had acquired through their new understanding because of their beloved Master.

Miriam got up and felt dizzy. She slowly approached the door.

John turned as she walked out onto the small terrace where they were gathered. They looked at each other. The young man immediately understood that she was full of holiness and that this would be the last time he would see her.

They all turned to her as they had done that morning when she brought them the incredible news. But now their faces were attentive and enlightened. They expressed a devotion that would never leave them again. It was an energy that would bring great change to the world. Without saying anything but their names, she embraced them, giving them a tacit blessing for the particular path each one would take.

When she stopped in front of Peter, the fisherman's deep eyes filled with tears. Despite all his doubts and the problems he had given her, he respected her deeply. He knew that the Master was part of her. He knew that when he embraced her, he embraced him as well. He whispered "Forgive me" as he held her in his arms for a long time and felt Miriam's forgiveness penetrate into him.

Once again, he felt redeemed. His conscience perceived that she, whom he had been so wary and jealous of, accepted him completely because she was made of real goodness. That forgiveness was absolutely liberating and regenerating.

Miriam had given her pure love to others so many times, often at a high price by accepting the suffering they had caused her unjustly.

It was one of many aspects that emphasized the overcoming and defeating of her ego through self-transcendent kindness. Some people had hurt her so deeply that the scars from those wounds would never disappear. Miriam had learned to put all things into God's hands, to let go, and to accept what had to be when she knew she had given her all. She had also forgiven those whose behavior had been particularly harmful because she knew what consequences would inevitably occur and she felt pain and regret for what would happen to them. On several occasions, those who had committed an unjust and terrible act against her and the purity of her heart suffered terrible consequences, even unintentionally fatal ones.

Peter knew what he had to become, the importance of the role he had to play in the future for Joshua and his mission. To do that, he had to find coherence between his inner being, his thoughts and his actions, and not being sure that he would achieve this state of transparency, he wanted to take the first step in relation to her. Being purified through her unconditional forgiveness would free him.

Miriam wanted to give him this chance. It was the greatest gift she could give him before she left.

After those intense farewells, Miriam headed to the center of the city. She was no longer alone, as she had been until those three intense and transformative years with Joshua. Her steps were quick and certain as she approached the beginning of her mission... of their mission.

Miriam quickly crossed the dark and narrow streets. She knew she had to hurry because the risk was very high and it was crucial that she leave Jerusalem and Judaea at the beginning of the day. An immense feeling of emptiness was rising within her, creating a great abyss in the center of her being. She had managed to keep it at bay all that time with pure willpower but the sense of abandonment was gaining space within her. She knew that their physical separation was part of the success of the plan, she had joined and participated in its creation, but now she would have to reckon with her human reality. To deal with this pain she would devote the rest of her life to prayer and solitude.

She felt that tears were beginning to fall regardless of her will. There had been a time when she had believed that nothing in the world would ever separate them. Losing the presence of those who are loved more than life itself gave her a melancholy that was spreading through every fiber of her being and she understood that this emotion should not reach the life she carried in her womb, she had to find the strength to face everything no longer for herself.

Something magical happened, she felt it inside her, and she knew that he would be with her forever, even beyond this life, as a great light in her heart and soul.

She walked even faster now, and the tears streamed down her face, but they had become tears of joy.

"Yes, I can hear you, you are in me!!! "she heard herself cry out.

At that moment, she remembered the voice when it had told her what the antidote was to every pain: Surrendering herself in his arms, certain of his love, in the same way that she surrendered totally to the will of God.

"Thy will be done!" she said from the depths of her soul, the same words that Joshua had said in his moment of hesitation, when his heart felt split in two at the thought that he must leave her for the sake of humanity.

The tears stopped. Peace filled her soul like a rising sun. Her forces returned, invincible. She had accepted this path in devotion to her holy man and to her child.

The tears would return, but not in this life.

She found herself in the marketplace. It was empty and silent, in stark contrast to the noise and activity that had filled it hours earlier. The uncertain light of a waning moon filled the empty spaces with a pale, bluish light. She raised her eyes to the sky. The stars shone brightly, encouraging her with their gleam, giving her strength through the darkness like countless candles. She felt a deep peace come over her, despite the danger she was in and the need to leave the city as quickly as possible. She felt protected and guided.

Here was the real Miriam, strong and ready for everything that awaited her. The decisions they had taken together were focused in a single will and singularity of purpose. She was no longer afraid because she no longer doubted. She knew that she was in God's hands, as she had always been.

She looked at the moon and it seemed to her that it smiled at her as complicit and intimate as that night, their last night together in the garden ... the garden of Gethsemane. As she was crossing the market, the silence that surrounded her made room for her memories.

The olive trees seemed motionless, embraced in the light of the moon, creating a play of light and shadow similar to static dances along the avenues of the garden. At a certain distance, in an adjacent grove, two silhouettes seated next to each other looked like one body only in the moonlight.

"It must happen tonight," Joshua said softly. "The time has come."

Miriam did not answer. She knew that this, too, had been written a long time ago.

"Everything is ready," Joshua continued, "Judas has agreed to do as I asked."

"I knew that he would," Miriam exclaimed. "Even if it will cost him his life because he is ready. He is the only one of them who can understand."

Then she added in a soft voice: "His devotion to you and to what is to be achieved is unparalleled. When he told you, 'I know who you are and where you come from,' I knew that it was true."

"No one else will ever understand except you," he added by putting a hand on her cheek and looking at her with eyes full of love. "He will be insulted...and so will you... like all those who have eyes to see."

"And ears to hear ..." she concluded, repeating the words she had heard so often.

"The brothers cannot give more and we cannot risk everything being lost. There is only one way to be sure. "

"What is that?" she asked, uncertain.

"The fruit of our love will be the guardian of the truth and will perpetuate the mission in the future. It is the only way to guarantee to the world its survival".

"It could mean more persecution..."

He took her hand and held it tightly. She felt the familiar warmth that emanated from him entering her body.

"Yes, that is why the seed must remain hidden from the world. It will spread silently. "

Miriam's face turned radiant.

"An incarnation of our love..."

"Imprinted in the blood, more powerful than any word or memory," he said with certainty. "It will be a tangible manifestation."

They walked hand in hand silently in the shade of the olive trees.

"You are the cup that will carry the fruit into the future, Miriam."

"All I wanted was to love you... That is why I was born. God's will be done!".

They stopped in a small clearing surrounded by trees, hidden from the world.

"Finding you was for me the greatest miracle of all," Joshua said, keeping her close.

They hugged each other for a long time. In that embrace of supreme love, they seemed lifted beyond time. The moment was eternal.

He laid his cloak down on the grass and helped her to sit beside him in the shadows.

"Don't be afraid, not a seed will be lost," he whispered in her ear. He took her face in his hands. "You are a warrior of light, my little Miriam."

"I will bring our love into the eternity of my soul," she whispered with a gaze that seemed to come from the infinite.

"I will be with you all the time... and beyond. Be sure of that."

Her eyes shone with tears despite her best efforts not to betray her pain.

"I will seek you...from life to life. I will never leave you. Although I will have to come to you through the form of another man. You will recognize me and we will be Three in One. "

Miriam remembered what her father had taught her a long time ago. Little Mira before the triangle of the Holy Law had now become its cosmic manifestation. Joshua had given her the key to an eternal, transcendent yet immanent love to open the doors of all the worlds she would visit.

She had skillfully planned everything with him, accepting the pain that would endure beyond this life because she knew he would be with her in many other ways, as the inner voice that would never stop talking to her, in the dreams that pointed the way for her, or in the pure souls that would love her from life to life beyond all limits.

They stretched out on the ground fresh with dew. At that moment, only one thing mattered, that they were still together, that they could still look into each other's eyes and feel the physicality of their bodies and their mutual warm breath.

He kissed her with all the sweetness and passion he possessed. It was more than a kiss, it was pure alchemy, the union of two bodies of light that would make them one, transmuting them into a new being forged in Athanor by the divine fire of a love, creating not only a new life but regenerating every cell of their bodies. This was the greatest

153

miracle he had performed because it was a miracle that renewed when two beings choose to belong completely to each other and to become one, merging with the source of all existence. When the Holy of Holies reached the peak of this supreme moment of ecstatic self-giving and complete receptivity, time and space dissolved. The stars, the trees, the sounds of the night gave way to a sacred symphony inaccessible to impure human beings.

Now she had become him and he had become her, as in the beginning. From this sacred mystical fire, something of the eternal good entered the third dimension beyond time and space, flowing silently through the progress of humanity.

The crickets stopped chirping, the nocturnal birds ceased whistling, and the breeze settled down in the leaves. For a moment, nature became silent, as if it wanted to timidly leave them in total intimacy. The love they shared opened onto the kingdom of heaven and the angels themselves closed their eyes, smiling and silent. The moment was too sacred even for them.

Under the full moon over Gethsemane, Miriam and Joshua celebrated for the first time the communion of the living gathered in the heart of God.

They had the key to the heart of the universe because theirs was an exclusive love that transcended opposites by bringing them beyond space-time when the vibration of light had not yet been created.

There, in the small garden on the Mount of Olives overlooking Jerusalem, the fabric of the three-dimensional world opened a door to the Eternal, revealing its presence.

The being born of their union would bring to the world the experience imprinted by atomic radiance through the organic, metaphysical and psychological elements of this sacred couple for the spiritual evolution of humanity. Where the writings could vanish or be misinterpreted, this presence in flesh and blood would establish the real perception of oneself and the meaning of life. Slowly, over the centuries, the truth would spread more and more until the children of God would see the world through unconditional love, recognizing themselves in him.

Miriam, who could see in the distant past her previous incarnations and perceive with great precision the events in progress, knew that the pain of separation in the depths of her being would re-emerge in every life through which she would travel. She would always be looking for such love, knowing that she would find it one day as promised. The man who would open himself to such love would be completely transformed and saved.

Joshua had promised her that the day would come when they would reunite through human love and that they would be three in one again, finally finding healing for that pain.

With her mind and heart immersed in this whirlwind of memories, Miriam arrived at the pier outside the walls of the great city.

She was to meet a man she had known since childhood, whose knowledge stemmed from his deep interest in absolute truth, from the teachings that had engaged him all his life, and for whose cause he had invested his finances. Despite his status in the religious community, in which he had an authoritative role, he risked everything to support them. Now, as always in secret, he would also participate in the development of their project, but in a new way. There was no longer any need for cash gifts or for the family tomb to receive his tortured body to be transferred and cared for, bringing it back to life. He would personally take Miriam to the next chapter of her journey, according to plan. He would help her leave Jerusalem for the western lands where the seed would blossom.

Joseph of Arimathea was a powerful man in his physical presence. His sharp mind had led him to develop a successful business in Gaul and Britain, trading oriental spices and other raw materials. His visionary thinking had opened up new avenues of trade and it was along these roads that Miriam's destiny was to be brought.

With his dominant personality, he reminded her of her father. They had been good friends, sharing both spiritual and commercial interests. After the premature death of her father, Joseph had become like a second father to her, attentive to her well-being, and he tried to guide her into a life that seemed uncertain because of her personality. This was not an easy task as Miriam was by nature so independent, strong-willed and rather rebellious. Her deep mind and intuitive powers made it difficult for her to let others tell her what to do. Her freedom to be in the place that corresponded to her desire was fundamental for her. From life to life, her romantic relationships would be shaped in the context of that freedom. Joseph also knew that she was not like the others and that he had to let her be who she was, regardless of the risks.

For a man used to giving orders, this was an important new experience. Powerful men bowed to his desires and he had not met anyone who dared to challenge his imposing presence. Yet this young woman, with her sweet innocence and purity, had opened his heart and the great man, through her, let emerge another part of himself, a vulnerable aspect of his soul that very few saw or could imagine.

For Miriam, he became not only a father figure, but a reliable friend, a confidant, one who supported her unconditionally. When she went to see him and told him about the young rabbi, she knew he would take risks like never before. He had felt the anger and hatred of the Synod and tried to appease his Pharisee comrades and other community leaders, not only because he knew there was something new and unique about Joshua, but mostly because he wanted to keep Miriam out of danger.

She was the daughter he had always wanted. All his power, wealth and importance in the community were nothing compared to the joy she could give him. To be useful to this precious human being who, by the grace of God, had become part of his life was now his mission. It gave him more satisfaction than anything he had ever done. She was like a little bird of paradise fallen on his balcony because she could not fly yet, sent by God to give him the opportunity to express all the love in his heart. He loved her, wherever she was, even when far away, in a manner he could not imagine possible, and this was his true salvation.

Miriam found him waiting for her in a secluded corner of the pier near a small boat prepared for a long voyage.

"Are you all right?" he asked in a deep voice from under his long grey beard.

She nodded silently and his stoic face softened, as was always the case when he laid his eyes on her.

"I know that it is very difficult to leave behind everything you love..."

"No, it's not difficult. Not after ..."

He knew what she meant. Not after him. To Joseph, it seemed unimaginable that he would never see them together again. They were perfect together, as no other couple.

"There are blankets waiting for you. And food. You will have to stay here tonight, hidden, I will come back with the others before dawn. We will leave immediately. "

She smiled at him with gratitude.

"I'll keep you safe, Miriam," he couldn't help but say. She hugged him gratefully and walked towards the boat.

The sun rose over the waters as on the first day, through a mix of rich tones that faded between orange, red and purple on the horizon. The sails fluttered festively in the morning breeze as the small boat glided forward with the tide, making its way against the gentle foamy waves that sprayed upward, blessing its wooden side.

Miriam, unlike the others, sat at the bow, her eyes fixed on the glorious rising of the sun. She saw in creation all the goodness and perfection of God and was grateful for the purpose of her life. She felt strong and serene, certain to be in his hands, just as when she floated on the waves as a child in tune with a greater reality. Now the waves and the wind were pushing her towards an unknown future, yet full of promises for the fulfillment of her destiny in this life. Her faith had never been so vast and luminous, like the dawn that unfolded before her.

She closed her eyes for a moment and whispered the prayer that her beloved grandmother had taught her and that was always in her heart: "The power of God surrounds me, the might of God purifies me and I am protected here now and forever from everything and from everyone: It's true!!!".

As the golden globe rose into the sky, the little ship headed toward the open ocean. She would need to fight for the new life that was in her, and the small splashes of the waves against the hull that sprayed her face made her feel alive and strong. In the whisper of the wind rippling through the waters with its salty scent from faraway lands and dancing in her hair, in the comforting warmth of the sun rising from the multicolored clouds with the promise of a new day, Miriam heard his words echoing loud and clear in every atom of this vision of supreme beauty: "I will be with you always, to the end of time."

The End

Epilogue

by Jess Nottinghill

I had recently read a very interesting article full of information and reflections that was entitled:

"According to some scientists the science of premonitory dreams is possible!"

Among other things, were written these words:

"-Jung says that there are great dreams in which it is possible to come into contact with energies of an "archetypal" nature, guardians of those primordial, innate and inherited data of the human mind that put us in a position to predict otherwise unexplained events with only the elements of the individual life of those who dream".

and again

-"According to Greg Braden:

During the premonitory dream the spirit frees itself from matter to proceed on the paths regulated by the universal space-time rhythms. It is from these journeys and from their "universal" information that the intuitions of the premonitory dream derive."

And I know very well that:

"-Many dreams and visions described in the Bible are of a prophetic nature: Joseph receives in a dream the news of Mary's conception of a supernatural nature; it is in a dream that God warns him to flee to Egypt; in the book of Genesis God speaks to Jacob in a dream, showing him the ladder that extends to Heaven."

But how do you react when an email arrives from the other side of the world describing both you and the place where you are because it is the fruit of a dream...?

I didn't answer!

I started receiving letters anyway, which clearly were not expecting an answer!

The person who wrote to me was a woman with a very special soul.

She wrote an email every day for five months, about 150 of them, in which she revealed to me her life, her thoughts, her intuition, her mystery and an extraordinary depth of love that I had never seen before.

I had been studying these themes for over forty years, but the psychological and spiritual intuitions of these letters amazed me and attracted my curiosity in an indescribable way. These letters were of such depth, poetry and spirituality that they changed my life.

Perhaps they will be published some day because they deserve to be shared with the world.

Why haven't I responded all this time? I have often asked myself this question, but thinking about what was revealed to me in those letters teased my nature as a researcher and writer more than that of a man. Her letters caused me to undertake a journey of research that lasted two years. I put all the skills of a lifelong scholar of religions and sacred writings into this journey. I had to discover and confirm what I had immediately guessed about who "Ella" was.

During this research, I discovered a life full of spiritual and paranormal experiences in the midst of the drama and joy of a common human existence. How did he know the things she knew? What were the origins of these profoundly sensitive spiritual perceptions? Every clue led me to travel through the lands of her childhood and youth, to discover other mysteries.

From all this the book "The Tree of Mira" was born.

What I finally discovered was not something that could be put into a simple sentence. The confirmation of who actually hid in this woman could only be shared with her as the result of my journey, through this book that was born from the experiences of these two years. What I learned was too significant to be expressed otherwise because that exploration of her life and experiences changed me radically, changed my understanding of religion, changed my relationship with God. By discovering who she is, I discovered who I am and my role in her life, and the true purpose of our meeting.

Ella closed the book and, while her heart continued to beat rapidly, she quickly readied herself. The puzzle was completed and the tangle of emotions within her exploded in a rainbow of energy.

This revelation was powerful for her, because it was familiar, intuited, and deliberately ignored for a long time. She had had multiple confirmations throughout her life before the appearance of the book she held in her hands which authenticated them through "scripta manent," written words remain.

An important memory returned, dominating the eye of her mind.

She had to leave the north to follow her youngest daughter who fell in love with a boy from the capital. Benedetta still needed her presence.

It was a difficult but necessary decision, to renounce to her beloved and rediscovered sister Anita, with whom they had cried for a long time embracing each other in recognition, to her trusted friend Grace, confidant and wife of a man very important to Ella, an ancient brother of faith and intent who had introduced her with great delicacy and respect for her true identity, on which she had never wanted to dwell so much, while walking in the evening through the semi deserted streets of a mysterious and magical Milan.

In Esther, the great writer who had introduced her to her small group of friends, intellectuals of God, protecting her from worldliness, in a role that was a distant reverberation. To her beloved Sirius, writer and once a distant member of the Sanhedrin, custodian of its most intimate secrets.

A few years had passed since she met the woman who was to become her best friend in this new and eternal city.

They had arranged to meet for coffee in a small square in the heart of the "Eternal City." It was the first time they had seen each other after the evening of presentations in which they had immediately sympathized. She had no clear memory of her appearance and, being early as usual, she entered the church of the Saint to whom the little square had been dedicated for a brief prayer.

She loved the quiet and sacred atmosphere of ancient churches, embellished by the sculptures and icons of important artists. She felt intimately at home in the peace that emanated from this mystical space, with its half-light illumined by candles and imbued with the aroma of incense which she loved to breathe in deeply, because with every breath it seemed to bless her inner temple.

She had lived many special and unforgettable moments in sacred places since childhood, having grown up in a devoted and practicing Christian family, so the atmosphere of churches was a place where she found her loved ones with joy.

It was in places like this that she had been spiritually initiated towards a path of purification and transformation so evident and central in her art.

She walked quietly through the church, welcoming its silence and reverently lingering in front of the statues that surround her, in which a woman and her virtues were portrayed. There were few people present. An old woman in a corner was lighting a candle, another was on her knees in front of the Cross...

Then, she saw a young woman from behind, standing in front of one of the statues of Saint Mary Magdalene. She was clearly in prayer, a fervent and silent prayer that expressed all her need for comfort. After a few seconds, Ella seemed to recognize her as the person she was to meet.

Spontaneously and in a low voice she called her:

"Angelica...Angelica...".

The woman turned around, let out a shudder of amazement that resounded through the church, and said, "It's you!" in a voice full of wonder.

Ella was surprised to see the tears in the eyes of this woman she did not know well yet, happy to discover that she was the friend she had come to meet. Angelica embraced her warmly, as if they had always been friends, and immediately told her what had just happened, what divine action had taken place, touching her soul so deeply that tears of joy would come every time she would remember this moment in the future.

Angelica had prayed fervently to the Saint, asking at the height of her prayer for a sign: "Saint Mary Magdalene, please help me.... If you hear me, call me, call me, call me!"

At that same moment, Ella had pronounced her name....

In manifesting those words from the spiritual dimension in response to a fervent prayer, an extraordinary alignment occurred, making her the voice of Miriam, as if time had disappeared.

This incredible mystery sealed the new friendship and became a confirmation that remained in the secret places of Ella's heart, to emerge clarified now, through the book she held in her hands.

"It's you..." Those words resonated in her heart with a new power, emanating the light of an understanding that went through all the events and people of the life she had lived up to this moment. She felt her soul expand beyond time, beyond the confines of space, while still fully rooted in this moment of supreme meaning. A new inner force filled her being, a new sense of herself emerged, a new look shone through her eyes as she was putting on her make-up.

In the meantime, the daughters who had left her alone in respect for her privacy, had gone to a corner of the main room of the museum where they could talk undisturbed and observe the people who entered the exhibition.

Benedetta, taking the phone, suggested to Cristiana:

"We're going to stand over there, out of the room," she said, seeing a quiet corner away from the crowd. The sisters remained close as they looked at the phone.

"Do you think his name starts with a K or an N?" Benedetta asked.

"I'd say an "N", like in the Robin Hood story," and they laughed!

They watched the screen silently while the search engine did its job.

"There he is!"

"Look at all these sites and all these books..." Cristiana whispered, suspicious.

"How can this man know Mom?" Benedetta wondered.

"Scroll further down."

"He seems to have done a lot of things, historical writings, novels, spiritual material... A serious researcher," Benedetta said as she quickly moved her finger across the screen.

"He's a busy man...". Cristiana noted, "He won't have much free time...What is his nationality?"

"Let's see..."

"Try Wikipedia... or Amazon."

"Here he is..." Benedetta said with excitement. She was enjoying this investigation as though it were a game.

"American!" Cristiana said out loud. "I could have guessed. Americans are so...determined!"

"It seems that he grew up in Europe...".

"Then he should know the etiquette and not bother mother on the day of her biggest event! See if you can get an idea of this man."

"In images...Why don't I see any pictures of him?" Benedetta wondered.

"It's not a good sign," muttered Cristiana.

"Everyone has images on the internet... Let me check the back cover of one of her books."

"I knew there was something that felt wrong to me," said Cristiana with certainty.

"No, he has symbols or castles on the back...there's also Rennes-Le-Château.".

"Oh great, just what was missing, a conspiracy theorist!"

"He looks more like a spiritual writer than anything else," said Benedetta as she watched people enter the room. "We can't continue to do this here. It's not polite."

"We need to know more," said Cristiana looking around, as if she was seeking for answers around her.

At that moment, she saw a young man passing in front of them. He was rushing into another room.

"That's the young man who came to deliver the book!" Christian said with certainty and she chased after him immediately.

"Wait! "All she could do was follow her sister who was going straight to him.

"Excuse me," said Cristiana, "you brought a package to the artist a few minutes ago."

The young man stopped and seemed not to remember.

"You gave me a package upstairs for my mother, the artist," said Cristiana again.

"Yes...yes, I did," he exclaimed.

"Who gave you that package?"

"Do you remember who asked you to bring the package to our mother? "Benedetta asked gently.

The young man looked around and said:

"It's that tall man standing in front of the painting, Yes, it's him!"

The sisters looked in the direction in which he was pointing. A tall man, dressed in dark brown with a small ponytail, was standing in front of one of their mother's large paintings.

"Don't stare at him," Benedetta advised her sister.

Cristiana couldn't help but study him.

They moved through the crowd trying to get closer to him.

"What is he doing?" Cristiana asked.

"He is studying our mother's work," Benedetta replied.

"He's studying it very closely," observes Cristiana, "maybe he's also a critic or a journalist."

The Greek-profiled man, with his medium-length, grizzled beard, stood motionless in front of the big picture, looking at it carefully. On the wall nearby was the title "Even Horizon: Sky A." The brochure said that it was a dynamic contemporary painting that seemed to be in motion, full of small detailed images partly hidden in the background. He turned the page of the brochure, found an essay by the author about the work that had so caught his attention, and read:

The Event Horizon is a real point from which one could hypothetically observe the Past, Present and Future at the same time, as confirmed by scientists.

Before matter (understood as energy mass) can be sucked in by a Black Hole, Time slows down to such an extent that it stops at the edge, near the abyss.

Being able to observe events confers a great power of action, and to do so from the Event Horizon makes it a unique feature of the Evolutionary Synthesis, offering an intimate opportunity to play the role of Co-CREATOR through the experience of the ONE.

Since it is not possible to be eyewitnesses to this magic, we can simulate the experience by using techniques of imagination and visualization.

This personal experience of mine has allowed my inner vision to open a gap in the darkness of the mind towards a new and real energetic dimension in which, from the invisible worlds, forms and colors, characters and myths of the history of the world and of other worlds have emerged, giving rise to the creation of the following works...

He looked at the picture again...then he kept reading:

Humanity in its progress needs such a vision because the experience, transferred to the neurons, (represented in the works by the red filaments) would be imprinted in the DNA, becoming an invaluable wealth for the Terrestrial Genetic Heritage.

It would greatly contribute to the evolution of the species, in the acquisition of a broad and immediate visual communication, aimed at fraternal cosmic cooperation in the Universal Superior planes.

Her stellar origin was increasingly clear to him. A combination of such intuition, artistic ability and mystery had brought him into the presence of a complex and evolved being who expressed herself through art. He would never meet anyone like her again and he could hardly contain his excitement. He returned to the painting, looked at the dark green background, and saw explosions of thin red lines crossing the canvas along with numerous figures painted in softer colors. The man seemed completely absorbed by what he was looking at and, as his eyes moved slowly down the painting, he saw partly hidden within an explosion of a lighter color, a chalice from which all the red lines came. A chalice...? The Chalice!!! ...Under this chalice, he saw the face of a man with a beard and long hair who could only be Joshua and he thought: "I knew it...!!!".

The man's face also reminded him of another important person in these last two years.

He was in Greece when he read the name of the monastery where he was staying in an e-mail he received from an unknown sender. He realized that this was a mysterious and extraordinary coincidence. The tiny monastery was hidden on a small island in the Aegean Sea, so secluded that tourists had never come to visit it unlike many other monasteries scattered on the shores of the various Greek islands. How did this woman know of it and connect it to him? Originally it had been a hermit's cell, a place of peace, whose deep quiet was interrupted only by the solitary cry of the seagulls, a perfect setting for a writer. He had stayed there for several weeks because it was near the island of Patmos, a key place for his next book. He had written many books in recent years, always doing meticulous research on the subject he was dealing with.

He had arrived in New York with no more questions, and looking at the large painting entitled Sky A, he remembered sitting in the small, barren room where he was staying on the island, looking out the window and wearing the same jacket as he had on this day. He had just arrived at the monastery carrying with him his inseparable computer and a small leather suitcase. His beard was not too long yet and his ponytail gave him a fascinating air. He stared with the same attention at the images, colors and symbols of this great painting which, together with the other works, put an end to his mission. He had tried to isolate himself to write the new book on the end times, and could not think of a better place to start. Patmos was visible when he was sitting at the small table under the window, and even when the sun was setting, he could still distinguish its shape in the distance.

An image in the painting reminded him of the monk who had helped him.

Should he thank fate or Father Alexis for his being here now?

He had been in correspondence for a long time with the abbot of the nearby monastery, Father Alexis. It was thanks to his kind efforts that he had found the perfect monastery and was allowed to live there for a few weeks. The monk assured him that he would visit him whenever possible. With his long white beard and the typical black tunic of Orthodox priests, Father Alexis was a perfect representation of the spirituality of those places. He was a profoundly humble and cultured man, but how could he tell him that he had been researching writings rejected by the Church for centuries?

It was Father Alexis who introduced him to the Oral Tradition handed down in the monastic world and coming from the deserts of Egypt and the great mystics because he wanted to understand everything that had given life to the Book of Revelation.

Father Alexis told him that one of the apostles had visited this island and spent time on the grounds of this same monastery. He was very curious about this and wanted to absorb the atmosphere and energy of the place. When his friend informed him that he could have internet access on the remote monastery, he immediately booked a flight. A scholar of the Dead Sea scrolls, Gnostic writings and ancient mystical treatises, he felt at home wherever he could enrich his knowledge.

What an unforgettable moment was that familiar sound from his computer which told him that he had received an e-mail...even as he was so absorbed in his thoughts.

In the meantime, Cristiana and Benedetta realized that the curator of the exhibition was moving through the crowd, looking anxiously to see if the artist was in the room. They heard him say "where is she?" and they understood that their mother had to come down now because the journalists who had gathered around her paintings had many questions to ask her.

Cristiana and Benedetta ran up the stairs, realizing that it had been an hour since they had come down to investigate the author of the mysterious book.

Ella appeared at the top of the stairs just as her daughters were coming.

"Mom!" Benedetta exclaimed with a big smile, "how beautiful you are!"

"Why did it take you so long to get ready?" Cristiana asked, also happy to see her as usual in her best "appeal".

They came to her side to be the first to tell her: "Congratulations, yours works are awesome!!!"

"I have to tell you something," said Ella sweetly. "It's important!".

Her daughters knew that they needed to listen carefully regardless of the circumstances.

"I need to talk to you about that dream...".

"Okay, Mother, I get it, we can't do it later!" replied Cristiana, no longer anxious to take her downstairs.

"The voice told me to go to the monastery dedicated to the Virgin Mary...because I would find them the man of my life!

I found myself visiting it, opening all the doors, looking at the icons and walking in silence with great respect and devotion. I opened a new door, felt embarrassed and immediately apologized to two orthodox monks in their long black clothes, with their typical headgear and long beard, sitting next to each other intent on talking. They turned simultaneously toward me. One was old and the other young. No!!! My man a priest, nooo!!!! I thought in the dream!!!! The young priest asked me to wait, then he quickly said goodbye to the old master kissing his hand and walked towards me, taking my hand and we left the monastery. I knew when I woke up that I had to investigate because what the Voice says has always been unequivocal!"

She placed her hand on the handrail of the staircase to support herself from the emotion.

"Then what happened?" Benedetta asked in a whisper.

"As soon as I woke up I went on the internet to look for that monastery and find some clue. I searched through many images until I found only one monastery with that name, near Athens. I looked at all the photos that concerned it, but saw no interesting ones. Then, to my astonishment, I found one that portrayed two monks exactly as in my dream. Trying to open the image more than once, I opened the page of another man with a beard. I read his name and searched for him on Facebook. When I opened his social page there was only a photo of a monastery and it made me breathless! Without even a moment of hesitation I sent him a private message telling him about my dream, but without any expectation."

"And he replied to you?" Cristiana asked.

"No... he didn't answer."

"And then what?" asked Benedetta.

"I have to confess something to you...I looked for his email address because he is a known writer and I found him on the web. I started to write him an email every day for five months telling him about my life...".

The daughters looked at each other, amazed. Although they knew their mother's paranormal powers, the confirmations thrilled them with the same intensity. They turned again to Ella, who had a dreamy look in her eyes.

"Didn't he ever answer?" Cristina said with an annoyed tone.

She looked at each of her daughters.

"I just read the whole book that was brought to me...he is the author."

The daughters were not surprised to hear it.

"This book, after two years, this is his answer," she said.

In silence, the three began to descend the stairs, seized with emotion.

There were no words to add in this moment. They went down the stairs feeling ready and strong in the face of the onslaught of cameras and questions from admiring collectors and authorities present.

Ella and her daughters found themselves in the room where her works were exhibited and she was immediately surrounded by the crowd.

Ella answered all the questions promptly and professionally from her dedication to art, but this evening her answers were steeped in deep inner peace. The book had linked her to a dimension of her spirit that emerged with grace, naturalness and beauty.

While photos were being taken, a gap was created in the crowd. Ella turned around and her eyes rested on a man standing in front of her painting "Sky A". She looked at him with sweetness and depth for a long moment. Then the man turned and their eyes met. For a moment, everything vanished around them. There were only the two of them in that timeless look.

Someone brought her back to the moment by asking a question and Ella had to look away to answer the journalist. But she could feel her heart beating at a new pace, with a new type of ancient and familiar vibration. They looked for each other and smiled at each other with a complicity that seemed to come from the infinite.

Ella walked towards another one of her paintings with the guests at her side. Her daughters were so happy for her, knowing that, although she was in a special state, she managed to transcend everything in these public situations.

Slowly, the crowd became smaller and the event was successfully coming to an end. Seeing the people leave, Ella turned around looking for him again. He was there, looking at her, waiting for her.

At a certain point he smiled at her and felt that it was the right time to approach her. He leaned his head slightly forward and she gave him her hand to thank him for being there. He brought her hand to his lips and kissed it for a long moment. As he raised his head, his eyes saw the turquoise scarab at the very height of her heart, just as she had noticed the thin red silk cord appearing on his right wrist. They had the same thoughts, all the confirmations and answers they were looking for. The red thread was an important symbol in her life so as not to forget her origin, so much so as to make it a second signature on her paintings. The scarab was for him the symbol of the unresolved past waiting to find her and of rebirth from life to life. They felt their lives connected in a deeply mystical way.

As they looked at each other, her daughters asked her if she needed anything. "Just get my shawl, please... Thank you for existing, I love you!"

Her daughters went to retrieve the precious and soft Kashmir wool shawl that she had bought on one of her countless trips to India, from her beloved friend Bilal, Kashmir merchant, born in Srinagar in front of the temple of Roza Bal!!! They gently placed it on her shoulders.

"Do you need anything else, Mother?" Cristiana asked.

"That's all," said Ella with sweetness. "See you tomorrow," she said with a smile.

They hugged her and both whispered in her ear "we love you so much" and moved away, knowing that their mother deserved to have everything she had always wanted.

He took her by the hand, in a natural and spontaneous gesture. They walked towards the large door, leaving behind the big paintings that now belonged to the world, and that told their whole journey...perfectly described in 'HORIZON OF EVENTS!'

They went out into the cool night air of New York City, walking along the streets of the big city. The lights seemed to sparkle more intensely as they passed under the extraordinary September sky. Hand in hand, without saying a word, they moved into the future.

Everything was accomplished!

The Authors

Raffaella Corcione Sandoval was born in Caracas, Venezuela. She is a painter, sculptress, stylist and writer who currently lives and works in Rome. She attended three years of specialization at the Theological Faculty of the Jesuits in Naples 85/7, she traveled for 30 years in India deepening the Buddhist and Hindu philosophical thought. She has received many awards and has been published in many publications. She is an Artist known nationally and internationally. She established herself on the Italian contemporary Art scene in 2005 with the creation of the sculpture "Sindone Partenopea" (inspired by the Veiled Christ by the sculptor Sammartino) made of crystallized fabric, a technique she invented, exhibited during the great exhibition Il Velo, at the Filatoio di Caraglio 2006/7 with the greatest names in art of all time. Her works are part of private collections all over the world.

Theodore J. Nottingham is an author and translator of spiritual works who works in a variety of genres, including historical and metaphysical fiction, children's books, and non-fiction works on spirituality. He is also a video producer and has also been involved in the study of spiritual development for over forty years.

Interviews with the Authors

With Raffaella Corcione Sandoval

Q. You've been an award-winning artist for many years. What inspires you to create?

A. To receive an award is to have arrived in the heart of someone who recognizes the merit of having received an emotion as well as a concept to be explored.

An artist cannot specifically define what he or she draws inspiration from because he or she is the inspiration, creating is just the need to want to communicate.

You have experimented with many different styles and means, including now writing books. What is your opinion about the role of the artist in the world?

Every medium is a tool, there are no limits of styles or techniques, the results sometimes confirm the multifaceted ability of an artist who describes himself as the drop of an infinite ocean to which we all belong.

You use the language of symbolism in your paintings and sculptures, as well as in your poetry and prose, and even in your fashion design. Can you explain why communicating through symbols is so important to you?

The language is made of sounds to which we have associated graphic signs since the dawn of time, the synthesis contained in a symbol is a powerful psycho-gram that stimulates the perception of the observer and produces reactions and memories stored in our DNA.

You have been an artist all your life. Why are art and creativity so central to your way of life?

It's who I am and what I was born for.

You've done so many exhibitions, personal, collective, institutional. What would you like to do at this point in your life to continue sharing your art?

I feel full of enthusiasm and curiosity, ready to experience new and stimulating horizons that give me a sense of the finite and the infinite.

Who are some of the artists you appreciate the most?

They are many, from different eras and styles, to mention them would be limiting since every art form has encouraged me to express my individuality.

Art critics have never defined you by genre or style. You always seem to surprise them with new and unexpected work. How would you define yourself as an artist?

Simply an Artist.

What new horizons do you foresee for your work?

Every day is a new horizon, working on a project requires study, research, reflection and experimentation, it is not about time but bringing to completion what you believe in and starting over.

What led you to write the book "Ella"?

The need to share a part of me that no one could have ever known either through a psychological analysis or by describing chronological events of my life because it is extremely intimate.

Why a veiled biography?

The Veil is a mysterious element that makes the invisible accessible from the visible because it blurs its contours and minimizes the hidden truths.

Are the elements in the book real or fictionalized?

The Book Ella places itself exactly in the center, filtering the real which is too cumbersome even for me, with a fictionalized result.

Who were some of the spiritual Masters who guided your path?

I recognize in my life the privilege of having met many Spiritual Masters since childhood like St. Padre Pio who was even my father's spiritual father, meeting him often. I had the honor of being able to converse with elected souls such as Gustavo Rol, Mother Teresa of Calcutta, The Dalai Lama. To elect my Master Sri Sathya Sai Baba by meeting him in India for 30 years, to pray with Monsignor Milingo, Swami Roberto and many other lesser known souls.

Each of them planted a seed in my soul, making it a fragrant garden with the passing of "my time".

What do you hope the readers will learn or take away from this book?

What everyone is ready to receive, whether consciously or unconsciously.

How do you think your book will affect the spirituality of our time?

After the Coronavirus nothing will be the same as before, this is the time of the New Covenant with God and my book is just one of many candles lit in the Temple of Renewal.

In this book, you provide new insights into important teachings of the Gospels and the Gnostic Gospels. What are the implications for Christianity and for the seekers of God?

Ella was written by me and an expert in philosophical and theological questions, I have only answered h questions, on the unresolved questions. He is the one you must ask about Christianity and the Gospels. For the seekers of God everything is simpler because nothing escapes a pure heart and an attentive mind.

When did you first discover your paranormal gifts and this preponderant spiritual identity?

There was not a beginning but always a succession of sometimes uncomfortable confirmations.

Why do you share your book with interested readers online before it is officially published?

Because as never before, each one of us tries to support others with our own means and when a decision is made, that is the perfect moment for those who believe.

What is the next step for this project?

In addition to the publication of the book, which is currently translated into four languages, the project includes the possibility that there may be a producer interested in making ELLA a film, having also written the screenplay.

Are you also working on other projects?

I plan to publish a series of children's initiatic stories entitled "Hidden Fables" and prepare a solo exhibition for November 2020.

What is the role of Mary Magdalene in our time?

The role of every woman and mother of all times.

From your point of view, and in relation to what is happening in the world right now, what is your thought about the future of humanity?

The Divine took us by surprise despite the fact that we were all aware of the end of time, but notwithstanding this terrible moment, God's mercy mitigated the predictions of visionaries and saints and the salvation of the planet took over human wickedness. Man, having to this day committed the greatest sin, that of presumption, I believe that our children can begin to hope for their children a better world in which respect and protection of the Earth will take priority.

By Aldoina Filangieri

Interview

With Theodore J. Nottingham

Q) How did you and the Artist meet?

A) It happened thanks to technology in unexpected and extraordinary circumstances. Out of nowhere, at a particular isolated moment in my life.

How did the idea of writing this book together come about?

It was born from the inspiration to complete the Gospel of Mary Magdalene which was discovered in the late nineteenth century in Upper Egypt in Coptic translation from the Greek. Not published until 1955, due to the world wars and other factors, the first six pages are missing, as well as portions of chapters 4, 5, and 8. Two other fragments of the same material were later found, which is very unusual for such an ancient text, suggesting that it was well circulated among early Christian communities. We shared the intuition that the spirit and teaching of this writing was especially important in our time. I might even say that we felt a duty to complete it. The work expanded naturally and I feel that we were guided by a higher plan.

In the book you say that this meeting changed your life. What exactly are you referring to?

I discovered in Raffaella a depth of heart and soul that resonated in such a way as to initiate me into new levels of being. It was a spiritual and emotional evolution at exactly the right time of my life, and with her I found the answers I've been searching for during forty years of spiritual study and experience.

How do you think the Church will react to the answers in the book?

The very nature of the Church and not only her, from whatever Tradition, sets limits to the awakening of the human spirit within the confines of its particular creeds, rituals and hierarchies. This has always been the case and the great mystics have often been marginalized in their lifetimes despite the words of Christ: "The wind blows where it wishes, and you hear the sound of it, but cannot tell where it comes from and where it goes. So is everyone who is born of the Spirit." (John 3:8). I am certain that seekers of God across the world in our time will find teachings and perspective that will greatly benefit their journeys. We live in a historical moment of great transition for Humanity.

How did your personal spiritual journey lead you to this revelation?

I was profoundly influenced many years ago by the mystics of Christianity such as Meister Eckhart, St. John of the Cross, St. Theophan the Recluse as well as those of other Traditions. Enlightened contemporaries like Thomas Merton and Krishnamurti played an important role in moving forward on the path. In my twenties, I was deeply involved with the study and practice of the teachings of G.I. Gurdjieff and his Fourth Way approach to self-knowledge and the awakening of higher consciousness leading to our authentic Self. All this allowed me to recognize in Raffaella the manifestation of all the teachings I was studying.

You have written and translated many books. What are the central themes of your other books and how do you view this book?

All of my books deal with spiritual themes, whether they be historical fiction, visionary works, or non-fiction. The translations of Spiritual Masterworks, namely from Father Alphonse and Rachel Goettmann, two of the most enlightened people I have ever met, and Karlfried Graf Durckheim, the great German spiritual teacher and "father" of transpersonal psychology, deal with these perspectives and methods of openness to the greater Life. Readers will find in "Ella and the Tree of Mira", through Miriam's teachings to the Apostles and her interpretation of the Scriptures, themes that are perfectly integrated.

As a spiritual seeker and in the past also a Protestant Reverend for 40 years and in recent years almost an Orthodox monk, what impact has this encounter had on your knowledge?

My intensive studies of scriptures and spiritual writings, as well as the hardships related to the life of a Protestant Minister across all the years, along with the effort to assist others on their journeys, were foundational for the next level of development which could only be deeply personal. There comes a time when the books must be put down and the public teaching reduced so that the focus becomes introspective. The experience of meeting Raffaella was the next step to live in backlight the embodied experience of Miriam and Joshua's Unconditional Love. I can also say that all the knowledge acquired and personal efforts made have been enriched by the intuitive and emotional knowledge that resulted from this meeting.

The male character in the book is a writer who has made a great discovery. How much of you is there in what we find written, and if so, what criteria do you use to confirm its authenticity?

The discovery of who she is beyond time is entirely founded on the reality of who the Artist is in life. To come to a knowledge of this revelatory experience requires going passed the limitations of the mind and perceiving with the intuitions of the soul or the 'nous', as the ancients call it. The confirmations, or criteria, for this discovery are found in the testimony of what emerges from the depths of the soul and of what is incarnated in ordinary life. When every intuitive statement resonates with my forty years of study, expressed with stunning clarity and simplicity, and bringing to mind what Saints and Great Masters from all centuries have stated in the past, there is a recognition of a great mystery and awe at the spiritual level of knowing coming from a heart of exceptional purity and love for God. As an example, if a child where to speak of the laws of physics with an exactitude matching the discoveries of the greatest physicists, long before they could have studied these matters in school or read books concerning them, then it would be evident that this child was gifted with an intuitive knowledge that surpasses any logical conclusion other than that they came into the world with this knowledge already present within them. In a similar way, the spiritual and esoteric wisdom manifested in words and actions, reveal a depth of being that transcends this dimension and this lifetime.

The Artist says that she has answered your questions about unresolved issues in the Gospels. What do you think are the unresolved issues?

My understanding of "unresolved issues" might be better expressed as "fundamental ideas" that the human mind and soul have struggled with from the beginning of Christianity and continue to do so, perhaps even more, in our time. They are unresolved because the answers given over the centuries, mostly in forms of creeds, are either incomplete or do not resonate with the evolutionary need of the human soul. A writer once said that creeds are an attempt to express mystical experience in concrete terms and therefore cannot be understood without those personal experiences. For instance, questions such as "is Jesus human or divine?" or "why does wickedness exist?" or "how is the Son of Man within us?" or "what is meant by living bread" are given answers that integrate these teachings with our deeper Self rather than simply letting us believe as if it were just a matter of faith and dogma.

What do you think about the synchronicity of events as explained in the book and also about the fact that it appears in this moment of world pandemic?

The fact that this book and its revelations appears at such a moment without programming, suggests that it can contribute to this important time of renewal and clearer understanding of the message of the Gospels.

After Dan Brown's book and all the works that have been published on Mary Magdalene, what could this book add and what do you think was not known before?

It is now known that Mary Magdalene is the Apostle to the Apostles. What was not known before are her teachings and the expression of what Jesus imparted to her alone. The presence of Mary Magdalene is in this book. It is not merely information about her. This book also adds a new perspective on who she is in relation to Christ, not only in their human relationship, but in their spiritual equality and the integration of the masculine and feminine in the divine unity. In a way, one could say that this book gives the opportunity to discover her return to the world for the purpose of clarifying the original revelations.

The relationship between Jesus and Mary Magdalene remains controversial. What light does the book shed on their relationship? Are the scenes based on historical facts?

Their relationship is controversial only from a religious point of view which reduces the importance of the feminine, the fullness of Christ's humanity and unity with the Divine in all that it is. The historical facts, when considered without prejudice, point to the naturalness of their relationship but are not able to reveal the metaphysical dimension of who they are together. This is a lived experience, not an opinion and is part of the uniqueness of the book. It will be clear to the attentive and sensitive reader that the wisdom given here is beyond the confines of space-time, and the revelation of the relationship comes from that same source. It is eternal memory and present reality.

She presents the Gospel of Mary Magdalene in this book, which seems complete with the missing pages of the original manuscript, and presents new interpretations of

the Gospel of Thomas. **What sources did you draw from for this process?**

The source is the extraordinary mystery and depth of an intuitive wisdom that transcends the mind and is rooted in the heart, not only of this world.

The interpretations provided by "Miriam" on the Eucharist and other central teachings seem surprisingly original. What are the implications of the book for Christianity and the future of religion?

This book is an expression of that kind of revealed teaching that is needed for a future freed from the misunderstandings and limitations of the past. "I have told you this so that my joy may be in you and that your joy may be complete." (John 15:11)

The central character of the book is the artist who describes the meaning of her works in the exhibition. Is there a direct connection between the two female figures?

We can say that her works of Art are a continuous expression of this same consciousness.

Do you have other editorial projects together?

We have written six initiatory fables for children together which are being prepared for publication and we are working on a book that accompanies "Ella".

Is there a relationship between you and the artist as the book suggests?

The book is born from this mystical relationship and bears witness to it. It embodies a metaphysical love that cannot be expressed otherwise.

Who is for you Raffaella Corcione Sandoval?

Little Mira.

Reviews

Peter Hubscher
Marketing and Distribution Manager at Hepipress

The author is always a link between universes, a fragile crystal bridge that seems ready to break but is extremely resistant to the presumption of false interpretations.

The relationship or rather the bridge between our infinitesimal small and the infinitesimal large, the universe, is the result of our efforts to contribute to the recreation of the harmony of Creation. The perception of our contribution is that of a painter who places a point on a fresco, a minimal thing but, for an infinitesimal moment, allows him to look at the painting in reaction.
The painter does not see the dimensions of the work but is aware that his infinitesimal is the element that was missing in the completion of the perfection of the harmony of creation.

This harmony can also be defined as the result of love which is the aspiration of two or more souls to merge into One.

The love that we feel and that attracts us to our rediscovered part is the mystical process that brings harmony back into the universe and that wants to make us participate in this recreation of harmony.

The narration of the present, which seems to us already lived, is the confirmation that we have existed in previous lives and that we have a guide for future lives because tomorrow is nothing other than yesterday lived in different forms and therefore the subjects of our love are the spirit of the loves of yesterday that will become the loves incarnated in tomorrow.

We must overcome our desire for internalization which is nothing more than the fear of collaborating in the continuous recreation of cosmic harmony through our witness and our toil in the search, being aware of the immensity that can overwhelm us.

This is the season of Easter "In exitu Israel de Egypto" which indicates the passage from the state of humiliation and slavery that is the fruit of disharmony to the state of harmony through a path of purification which the texts narrate in symbolic form. This writing is the instrument that helps us on this path, ours can only be an individual search that leads us to confront truth that we only intuit.

The drive to research driven by forces that we do not yet understand makes us realize that the harmony of the universe is the result of the integration of opposites that define themselves as deficiencies or completeness. Let us take the essential principles; immobility can be defined as lack of mobility and vice versa. Love is measured by hate and masculine and feminine are reciprocated.

These last two poles are the true engine of the Universe. They attract each other as parts of a whole and we call this attraction love.

Human beings have glimpsed these principles, but as said, we think we are alone in the search. Perhaps. But the intuitive feel the obligation to communicate, to teach others how to travel the path. Narrating the present, past and future by highlighting which events have opened our sight we become, albeit in a microscopic dimension, adherents of the guiding spirits who in a cosmic dimension have attracted and possessed us.

Credit to the writer for intertwining the discovery of these truths with the warp of a fabric symbolizing a revelation of love that persists and is renewed in time.

April 2020

Shawn Williamson
Sculptor and Researcher to Dr. Andrew Sinclair

I know the Art of Raffaella Corcione Sandoval as did my mentor Dr. Andrew Sinclair.
This novel of metaphysical dimensions will take the reader on a multi-dimensional inner journey connecting, as Edmund Burke called it, "the great chain of the living and the dead." And like her Art, it is a gift for those who can learn to see beauty through spirit through her words.

April 2020

Maria Gabriella Lavorgna
President and founder of the non-profit Foundation "Il Mandir della Pace"

This book, by the author Raffaella Corcione Sandoval, from the very first lines of reading, highlights and unfolds in a fabric, imbued with an intense spiritual journey as well as the fruit of the knowledge of one's own Self, in the perspective of the logic of creation, drawn from the source of ancient Vedic wisdoms which allows access to Truths of a higher order than those acquired intellectually or culturally. I have known Raffaella for about 30 years, whose friendship is rooted and consolidated in recognizing each other in similar paths and parallel lives, so I can testify that this book is the "mirror of her soul", the bearer of subliminal messages that are intertwined in an alchemical fusion of symbolism and esotericism, in the encounter between " matter and spirit " to the integration of the opposites, in the crucible of the Universal Matrix of the " I am," and whose end corresponds to the objective of awakening consciences, obscured by the illusion of the separation from the One, interconnected and belonging to the great Human family as drops of the same Ocean!!!

April 2020

Dr. William J. Nottingham, Ph.D.
President Emeritus, Global Ministries

I am happy to comment on the imagined love affair of the Savior and faithful Mira. To think of possible intimate connection
based on the attraction of an elevated spiritual nature common to both is an inspiration to readers. Who can say what
the Disciples observed among their comrades? That the ordinary is changed into new life is true to the meaning of the biblical history and the power of God.
Beyond the theological is the mystery that weaves its own story of signs and symbols free from the literal tradition of Christian doctrine.
The blending of two books through the art exhibition in New York delineates legendary interpretations of Scripture with Essene folklore. This is liberty for the reader's religious imagination and mystical enjoyment.

April 2020

Printed in Great Britain
by Amazon